YEAR
OF THE
DEMON

I0640199

DAVID NORTH-MARTINO

Macabre Ink

A jangle of bells. Four men entered. They wore masks. Japanese oni masks.

Vance recognized them. His Japanese stepmother (his mother had died during childbirth) and Marine father had donned oni masks and chased him around the house.

Giggling, young Vance threw dry beans, scaring the oni away and inviting good luck into their home. For a time, luck was with them. It didn't last.

The demon-men wore hoodies and carried baseball bats.

Behind the counter, the proprietor raised his hands in supplication. The girl backed away from the counter.

Should he intervene? He was unarmed and outnumbered. Not to mention, he hadn't been feeling himself lately. Lately? He hadn't been right for at least a year.

"Give us the money," one demon demanded. The bright red festival mask moved in perfect articulation with his mouth, as if it wasn't a mask at all.

He slammed his bat on the counter, cracking the glass, making a display of butane lighters jump. A cup full of pens rattled on impact.

The cashier started. His shaky hands released the cash draw. Change made metallic music on the smashed counter as he scooped out the contents.

"Take it. Take it all and go."

"That's not enough money!" a demon said.

Another demon swung a bat, hitting the clerk in the head. Blood splattered, and he fell behind the counter.

Vance winced but did nothing. It was unlike him to freeze. He'd been trained to fight.

Another demon noticed the girl. "Hey, grab the chick. She's coming with us."

The young girl in the bright red leather jacket turned, darted into the maze of aisles. Strong hands yanked her backward. Vance met her eyes again. This time, they pleaded silently. All indecision receded.

Dedication

For Shoshanna… We remember.

Acknowledgments

This novel could not have been completed without the following individuals.

Deepest thanks go to David Niall Wilson, Trish Wilson, and David Dodd for taking a chance on this novel and their tireless efforts in getting it ready for publication.

Thanks goes out to Alan R. Warren for his friendship, mentorship, and endless encouragement.

I would like to thank all my martial arts teachers throughout the years for sharing their knowledge, lessons, and insights that informed the writing of this book.

My thanks go out to David DF Cotter and Susan Taylor for reading earlier drafts of this manuscript and their helpful suggestions that shaped the writing of this novel.

Finally, and most importantly, I would like to thank my wife, Patty, who has acted as my first reader, editor, and cheerleader. Without her love and sacrifices, this work would not exist.

Chapter One

Vance Palladian held the Korean sword, tip pointed toward his opponent. A drop of cool sweat traced from his forehead to chin. Andre Murphy stood on the opposite side of the mat. On the benches lining the walls of the dojang, Korean martial arts training hall, Vance's advanced students watched the standoff in anticipation. The dojang felt electric. What had he gotten himself into?

"Ready?" Murphy asked, twirling his bo staff in a figure-eight pattern.

Vance wasn't ready. He knew it. Murphy knew it. His top students knew it.

Vance nodded anyway.

Focus had been fleeting since Susan died. Maybe, just maybe, a little competition would jar him awake. Get him back to normal. One could hope.

Murphy advanced, a smooth confidence to his gait. Vance's students held their breath. They still believed in him.

Vance hadn't held a sword in years. Good old-fashioned unarmed basics is what he taught, just like his teacher before him. He shouldn't have accepted this challenge. Spirited sparing would have made more sense.

Murphy transitioned from twirling to thrusting. Vance parried a feint with the sword—barely.

"You can do better," Murphy said, swinging the staff again. This time lower.

Vance jumped, avoiding the attack, but couldn't recover in time. When he landed, the staff hit his shoulder and knocked him off balance.

Stay in the game, Vance!

He was drifting again. Back to when he'd found his wife. A botched robbery. A home invasion. The same type of event that had propelled him toward martial arts mastery. Her lifeless body. His agony.

The cops found the perpetrators. The murderers. Tied up nicely with a bow. Twenty-five to life. That should have satisfied him. Justice served. Only now he was alone. They hadn't had kids. Now there was nothing left. As if their relationship had never happened.

Newer pictures on social media. Old pictures in a scrapbook. He had never gotten along with his in-laws, and they were no comfort. He drifted away. Had it been a full year? He couldn't remember.

The pain of hardwood hitting his solar plexus, driving him to the ground, awoke him from his reverie. He couldn't breathe. Gasping for air, he stared at a stain spotted drop ceiling.

Murphy helped him up.

A collective sigh as everyone in the room breathed again.

"I guess I wasn't much competition," Vance said sheepishly.

Sarah Brody, Tim Mancuso's little girl, patted him on the forearm.

"It's okay, Mr. Paladin," she said, using his nickname. Much easier for the kids to say. "You'll get him next time."

Vance wondered if that was true. Maybe he was finished. He could try to move up in the security company he worked at bootstrapping his business. Maybe get into management. Vance gave her a wan smile. She meant well.

"Okay, show's over," he said, trying his best to sound authoritative.

He might lose a few students, but it wasn't the old days. Back then, if you lost a fight, you lost your entire school. Today, it was expected. You couldn't win them all. Nobody was superhuman.

"Line up," Tim, his top student, called out. All the students ran to their places.

They bowed out, and he shook each student's hand before they changed into street clothing and filed out.

Murphy hung back.

"I hope I wasn't too hard on you," Murphy said.

"Tough love," Vance said. "I need it."

"Just trying to get you back to normal, "Murphy said, his hands finding his hips. Murphy was defensive. He knew how bad a teacher defeated in his own school looked, and he was feeling guilty.

"Don't worry about it," Vance said. "They know I haven't been the same since Susan …."

"School doing okay?" Murphy asked, shifting his weight uncomfortably.

"I need a side hustle to make ends meet."

Vance looked around at the empty studio. The room reflected how he felt inside.

"You still need to get your master's rank," Murphy said, glancing at Vance's belt. "You've been doing this long enough."

"I've been dragging my heals. How's the kids?" Vance asked, trying to change the subject.

"They're good," Murphy said with a smile. "Love 'em so much it's worth putting up with their mother and her new boyfriend."

"Anybody new?"

"I'm seeing a girl right here in Little Rhody. You didn't think I came all this way just to visit you?"

"Well, go on. Get out of here. Go see your woman."

"You sure you're okay?"

"I'm fine. Just thirsty after your thrashing. I'll grab a Gatorade across the street."

The Quick Mart run had become a nightly routine.

"Before I leave, just in case you need to get in touch," Murphy said, handing Vance a business card. "Never hesitate to call me."

"You're in sales now?" Vance asked, looking at the card.

"Something like that," Murphy said with a wink. "Call the cell. The other number goes straight to the office."

"Thanks, man" Vance said. "Be careful. It's a bad neighborhood."

"And she's a bad girl," Murphy said with a wink. With a hearty laugh, he pushed through the door and out into the night.

A truck screeched to a stop, halogen lights blazing, allowing Vance to cross the street. He gave the driver a wave before entering the Quick Mart. The jangle of a bell as he entered. He nodded to the proprietor and headed around back.

A painfully pretty girl caught his eye. Asian. No older than twenty-one. She wore a black t-shirt with a green tiger on the front, cropped by a red leather jacket, and pour-on jeans that emphasized her figure. She had long, lustrous hair that must have smelled as good as it looked.

When their eyes met, he felt fixated. Green eyes that matched the silk-screened tiger. Contacts, he was positive. She glanced away, and he returned to reality. His face burned. A prickliness on his scalp-line as sweat broke out.

He exhaled a breath he hadn't realized he'd held. He followed her with his eyes as she headed toward the register.

Now he felt foolish. Just another guy giving her the eye. And an older guy at that. When had he become the older guy? As an athlete, thirty-five was over the hill. Yet, he didn't feel ancient.

Then came the guilt. What would Susan think of him? Maybe she'd be happy he was living again. When she was alive, he'd have gotten a swift kick in the balls. He smiled and sniffed back a tear.

Pushing away bitter-sweet thoughts, he grabbed a cold strawberry Gatorade.

A jangle of bells. Four men entered. They wore masks. Japanese oni masks.

Vance recognized them. His Japanese stepmother (his mother had died during childbirth) and Marine father had donned oni masks and chased him around the house.

Giggling, young Vance threw dry beans, scaring the oni away and inviting good luck into their home. For a time, luck was with them. It didn't last.

The demon-men wore hoodies and carried baseball bats.

Behind the counter, the proprietor raised his hands in supplication. The girl backed away from the counter.

Should he intervene? He was unarmed and outnumbered. Not to mention, he hadn't been feeling himself lately. Lately? He hadn't been right for at least a year.

"Give us the money," one demon demanded. The bright red festival mask moved in perfect articulation with his mouth, as if it wasn't a mask at all.

He slammed his bat on the counter, cracking the glass, making a display of butane lighters jump. A cup full of pens rattled on impact.

The cashier started. His shaky hands released the cash draw. Change made metallic music on the smashed counter as he scooped out the contents.

"Take it. Take it all and go."

"That's not enough money!" a demon said.

Another demon swung a bat, hitting the clerk in the head. Blood splattered, and he fell behind the counter.

Vance winced but did nothing. It was unlike him to freeze. He'd been trained to fight.

Another demon noticed the girl. "Hey, grab the chick. She's coming with us."

The young girl in the bright red leather jacket turned, darted into the maze of aisles. Strong hands yanked her backward. Vance met her eyes again. This time, they pleaded silently. All indecision receded.

As if moving through water, Vance stormed down the aisle. Heart thumping, mind racing, palms sweating. Nothing like the movies where the good guy defeated the bad guys without breaking a sweat. No. This was real life.

"Get your hands off her!" Vance screamed. His voice sounded strange to his ears.

Gross motor skills took over for fine muscle movement as he slipped into survival mode.

A vice lock on the girl's wrist. The demon stepped toward Vance, wagging the Louisville Slugger. The demon said something, but the words didn't register.

Vance only noticed the demon's exposed centerline.

Vance fired a side kick.

The kick connected, slamming the demon into the counter. The demon lost his grip on the girl and slumped onto the floor.

The girl stepped aside, her hands covering her mouth.

Another demon attacked with a bat. Vance jumped back, evading. Then, timing his entry, jammed in, trapping the demon's arms, delivering a bone crushing reverse punch to the ribs.

The punch pushed the demon toward the door.

Instinctively judging the distance, Vance jumped and spun, launching a sidekick to the demon's face. The demon rocketed into the door, knocking it open, tumbling outside onto the concrete.

Another demon. Vance skipped forward, hooking his heel over the next demon's shoulder. Connecting heel to temple. The demon shook his head to clear the cobwebs. Now a side kick into a jumping, spinning hook kick.

The demon slammed into the aisle, knocking over the display. A loud clatter as everything hit the floor.

Where's the girl?

Where's the other demon?

A flash of red in his peripheral vision.

He whirled around, centrifugal force increasing power, executing a back fist. Two large knuckles, hardened and enlarged from years of conditioning, met the demon's temple. The demon spun and hit the floor.

Was that it?

He had lost count.

A stab of pain erupted in his back—a knife? His head swam.

He saw a baseball bat. His vision doubled, then tripled.

He didn't have time to find an answer to his question. The bat came toward him. Consciousness left and all went black.

Chapter Two

Vance awoke to find a shadow standing at the foot of his bed. A blurry image without features. Lit from the window behind, he looked like he had wings.

Vance started in confusion, pulled at something attached to his arm, felt a searing pain in his abdomen, a burning in his groin.

The shadow walked to the bed. Vance's eyes slowly focused. The shadow became an Asian man. He wore a gray business suit. The banality offset by a red power tie.

"Easy," the man said. He lowered his hands slowly, palms down, a gesture normally used to pacify a wild animal. "Stay calm."

"Where am I?" Vance asked, his voice raspy, his mouth excruciatingly dry, a barren ravine stretching across his tongue and down his throat.

"You're in hospital," the Asian man said with a British accent.

Vance realized he wasn't just in a hospital room, but a private room. A room he couldn't afford.

"Do you know your name?" the man asked.

"Yes," Vance said. The word came out as a croak.

The British Asian grabbed a glass of water off a tray and brought the straw to Vance's mouth.

"Sip," the man said.

Vance sipped the liquid. The cold water hit his tongue and flooded his throat. True ecstasy.

"Vance Palladian," he finally managed.

"Good. I'll have the nurse update your chart," he said, returning the glass to the tray. "Your name is stronger than John Doe. Do you have a family you need alerted?"

The demons must have stolen his wallet.

"No. My parents died a long time ago," Vance said. Their memory filled him with both sadness and comfort.

"I'm sorry."

"Who are you?" Vance asked, "You're not a doctor."

"No one, really. Just a man. One who is extremely interested in the feat you pulled off, taking out four street punks. It was all over the news. The convenience store had video."

"So interested, you'd pay for a private room, Mr. —?"

"Shoto Maramoto," the man said. "I've been successful in business, and I have the means to help you."

"What do you want from me, Mr. Maramoto?" Vance asked, suspicion rising. Vance had rarely met someone who would provide so much out of the goodness of his heart. This man had ulterior motives.

"Sho. Please call me Sho. My friends call me that," he said. "You are not the trusting type. That's a good thing. Firstly, let me come clean. I'm here to thank you for saving my daughter's life."

"That was your daughter?" Vance asked. The violent events in the convenience store replayed in his mind's eye.

"Yes. You acted with bravery and courage. I owe you a great deal. But I'm afraid you're right. I want something more from you."

Here it comes.

"What more can I do?" Vance asked.

"I want to hire you to protect my daughter."

"How do you suppose I do that?" Vance asked, then chuckled. His throat hurt. "I'm not in condition to protect myself."

"No, I suppose you're not, but I can get you on your feet again relatively quickly. And I think you'll need the job."

"I'm a martial arts teacher. I don't need a job," Vance said, but how would he make rent lying in a hospital bed? How could he continue a side hustle?

"You can't earn much doing that. You're a man of conviction, your classes must be quite harsh."

"They were harsh, but gotta worry about litigation and keeping students. Most students today are hobbyists, not fighters."

"No matter, my offer stands." Sho turned to walk away, then thought better of it. "You defeated four armed assailants—experienced street fighters."

"Your point?"

"It's eating at you, slowly, insidiously. You'll think about it more as the days go by, as you heal. You'll wonder why, with all your training, you weren't able to defeat them without ending up here. And you'll wonder if I can coax something inside of you out, that could defeat even more."

"If you can do that, why don't *you* protect your daughter?" Vance asked, tiring of the game. But Sho was right. He would think about the attack for years to come. Perhaps, the rest of his life.

"I'm not young anymore," Sho said, leaning toward him. From a distance, Sho looked in his mid-fifties. The closeness dispelled the illusion and Vance could make out the lines and wrinkles above Sho's upper lip, and the deepening crow's feet that spoke of a man well into his seventies.

"And when I tied my sword, I didn't break the seal for my family. The way of the warrior is found in death, Mr. Palladian. For my family, I chose life.

"Whatever you decide, call me when you've healed," Sho said, depositing his business card on the tray. Then he made for the door without looking back.

"Wait, a minute! How long have I been here?" Vance asked, a panic growing within.

"A little over a year, Mr. Palladian. Happy healing," Sho said, leaving Vance dumbfounded.

Chapter Three

Vance spent the next six months in agonizing physical rehabilitation. First Sho sent an acupuncturist to treat him. Between the blood samples and the acupuncturist's needles, he felt like the proverbial pincushion.

Unlike the nurse's hypodermic, Vance never felt the pinch, only a slight pressure. Herbs burned on the heads. White smoke and subtle scents entered his lungs. He breathed in deeply while visualizing a fully restored body brimming with health.

Vance was no stranger to *muk yum*, meditation. A practice he performed to focus his mind and vitalize his body before and after every Tae Kwon Do training session.

Vance healed quickly, regained his appetite, had the catheter removed, could even get out of bed to use the facilities.

Then the real pain began. A physical therapist worked him over, and it was all he could do not to scream. To strengthen blood flow, the therapist performed deep tissue massage. Then Vance did scream.

On the morning of his release, Vance emerged into a grayish day, taking his first breath of fresh air in over a year. Wearing the freshly laundered clothing he almost died in a year ago, he felt like a convict released from prison. Where to go from here?

"Mr. Palladian?" a driver standing next to a black limousine asked. The driver was well-groomed. A young man of Asian descent, he dressed in a chauffeur's uniform and sported a subtle New England accent.

"Who's asking?"

"Mr. Maramoto sent the car," the driver said. "Come with me, please?"

"Tell your boss, I'll consider his offer. I appreciate his generosity."

"Where will you go? Do you have someone to pick you up?"

Vance didn't want to answer.

"I'll take you wherever you want. Give Sho a call if you're interested."

Vance checked his pockets again, found them empty.

Vance had little choice. Without money to hail a cab, he was out of options.

"I want to see my dojang," Vance said.

"Sho figured you might, but another business has already leased it."

Vance's shoulders slumped.

"Sho put your equipment in storage," the chauffeur said. "You didn't think the world would wait for you?"

"I suppose not. It was nice of Sho to retrieve my stuff."

Vance stood at a crossroads. He had been a martial arts teacher. Where would this new road lead?

"You don't look good," the driver said. "Jump in the car, fix a drink, and I'll take you to Sho. You'll have plenty of time to decide."

Vance turned, knitting his fingers behind his head, as if preparing to be frisked by police. He breathed deeply of the crisp morning air, regained some vitality, and spun back around.

"All right, Jeeves," Vance said. "You win."

"This is about you, Mr. Palladian," the chauffeur said, opening the door for Vance.

Vance eased inside the six passenger Lincoln stretch VIP sedan. The driver shut the door. One thing was for certain, Sho had class.

This wasn't your run-of-the-mill limo used for bachelor parties and proms. The Lincoln was decked out in finery: buttery leather seating, real cherry wood paneling, and a well-stocked bar. A console to his left displayed scalloped decanters filled with single malt scotch, fine cognac, white and red wine, water, and ice, along with rocks and wine glasses. Cloth napkin stoppers kept out contaminants.

Don't mind if I do, Vance thought. He scooped ice into a rocks glass and then poured three fingers' worth of cognac.

The chauffeur powered down the partition.

"I see you've made yourself at home," he said with a wink. "Good. Buckle up. It's the law."

Vance fastened his seatbelt and then sipped the cognac. The smooth liquid coated his tongue and pallet. Butter and honeysuckle. He could get used to this.

The young man eased the limo through the day's congestion. A breakdown cut off a lane on Route 95 and he took a winding detour to bring them past the slowdown.

"What's your name?" Vance asked.

"Kevin," he said, glancing into the rearview mirror.

"I'm Vance. My friends call me Paladin. My nickname."

"Paladin? I like that," Kevin said as he veered his car into the fast lane to pass a vehicle traveling under the speed limit. "Sho says you're a great martial artist."

"I appreciate that."

"Did you enjoy teaching?"

"Yeah, I did," Vance said, disinterested in the conversation. On a normal day, it thrilled him to talk about his work. This wasn't an ordinary day. Too many thoughts, too many questions. He had a lot to discuss with Sho.

"What?"

It took Vance a moment to focus on the question.

"What did I teach?" Vance asked. Kevin nodded. "Tae Kwon Do."

"Ah, Olympic style or the old Korean Karate? Either way, you guys are good with your feet."

"The old-style Korean Karate. It's not all feet," Vance said, feeling defensive. The Okinawan and Japanese karate styles liked to pick on their younger sibling, especially since it had become one of the most popular martial arts in the world among the mainstream public.

The visibility of the art, along with the convenience of location and the high profile of the Olympic games, brought hordes of children through the doors and produced scores of ten-year-old black belts. The ubiquitousness of children did little to support its reputation as a serious fighting art. Neither did the change to Olympic sport rules. Vance had trained in and taught a much older version of TKD when it was almost identical to Japanese Karate.

"No offense. Sho says you have an excellent foundation. One he can build on."

"Great. After eighteen years I've built a foundation."

"I think you'll be amazed with what you'll learn from him."

Yeah, maybe.

Vance couldn't believe Sho had super-secret training, making it possible to defeat a group of attackers and walk away unscathed. That was fantasy, not reality.

Vance tired of the conversation. He looked out the window as buildings passed and trees took their place.

Route 195 brought them to the Claiborne Pell Bridge, known to the locals as the Newport Bridge, a large suspension spanning the sparkling waters of lower Narragansett Bay. The water shimmered on either side of the structure.

Vance smelled the salt air even through the tinted windows. Rhode Islanders didn't like to traverse this bridge. Newport residents rarely trekked over, preferring the seclusion of stately mansions, cramped but quaint cobblestone streets, and sailboats.

Kevin ascended the bumpy incline, paid the toll in cash, and then descended directly into the Newport road system.

In short order, Vance saw bluffs and seawater, and mansions across the bay.

Kevin pulled off onto a private road and drove down the long stretch, a stone wall on either side pushing back trees, keeping the forest from reclaiming the space as its own.

Kevin slowed as they approached a wrought-iron gate with a uniformed sentry manning the guardhouse. Kevin powered down the window. The guard nodded his head and then opened the gate, allowing the limo to roll onto the grounds of the Maramoto estate.

The lawns and shrubs of the sprawling acreage stood perfectly manicured. The beautiful greenery on the hills and dales reminded Vance of a golf course, (he had worked for a summer as a laborer on one during his high school years) or, if he really wanted to romanticize, the Emerald City of Oz.

On the first hill, a beautifully constructed colonial mansion, the whitewash of the facade gleaming in the sunlight, dominated the estate and stood as an edifice of wealth and regality. Behind the mansion, a thicket of trees provided a dividing line cordoning off the property. Over a bluff, the open water of the Atlantic Ocean marked the other boundary. Yet, even these soft dividers made him feel more like a prisoner than a guest.

"Sho's a man of great taste, and great wealth," Kevin said. He pointed to a cottage just off the access road. "That's where you'll be staying."

"What? No mansion for me?" Vance asked and then laughed.

"Sho believes you need an austere life to complement your training. He thinks living in the mansion would be a distraction."

He doesn't want me around his daughter until he trusts me more, Vance thought.

"And if I do this," Vance asked. "Where will I be training?"

"Look to the right of the mansion. You see that structure on the second hill?"

"Looks like a Chinese teahouse."

"Looks can be deceiving," Kevin said.

"I thought you guys were Japanese," Vance chided.

"It came with the property."

Kevin pulled the limo in front of the cottage.

"We stocked the guest house with everything you need. I laid out your, well, you call it a dobak training uniform, we call it a dogi. Take a shower, get changed, and then meet me at the… Teahouse. The walk will do you good."

Vance found the door unlocked. The place was clean and functional, a dwelling you'd assign to a gardener.

His new abode sported a living room furnished with cushioned wicker furniture, a decent-sized stand but no TV, an eat-in kitchen, a cramped bathroom, and a modest bedroom.

Vance went immediately to the refrigerator and found it stocked. He pulled out a water bottle, cracked open the cap, and downed it. After a couple of adult beverages, he felt dehydrated. He threw the empty 16-ounce bottle in the trash bin.

First things first, Vance thought. He stripped off his clothing and tossed everything into the hamper outside the bathroom.

Inside, he looked into the medicine cabinet mirror. His haggard reflection stared back. After a year in a coma and months of physical therapy, he could look worse. He didn't look dead, maybe just half alive.

Rummaging through the cabinet, he found a bottle of ibuprofen. He swallowed two pills with a handful of water.

The water heated fast, and he took a lengthy, wonderfully steamy shower. He caught himself smiling. He hadn't smiled in forever. A tear slipped down his cheek, a small hole in the stony facade he had erected and clung to for months. And then he wasn't just crying, he was sobbing, purging him of sorrow.

He exited the tub sopping wet and grabbed a rolled towel from a wicker basket. After drying, he tied it around his waist, as if someone might see him. He felt like a guest here.

After a quick shave with a disposable razor, he entered the bedroom. The room contained a neatly made double bed and a dresser. On the bed lay a crisp white uniform, freshly laundered, and ironed, a pair of white Japanese tabi construction worker boots and his original black belt with gold Korean Hangul lettering that spelled Tae Kwon Do on the left with three gold stripes underneath, and Paladin on the right in English. The tattered belt his only link to his past.

Inside the bureau he found a package of athletic socks and boxes of runners' sweat-wicking underwear, two new pairs of jeans, tags still attached, and a black t-shirt, the ones that the celebrities wore, made with a small amount of stretchable fabric, along with a few other shirts of assorted colors. Everything looked like it fit. *What did Sho do while I was knocked out, take measurements?*

He suited up, slipped into the tabi, and then slung his belt over his shoulders. Gold's tradition had been to only wear the belt when ready. Replacing laughing, joking, and idle conversations with a quiet awareness and readiness for whatever training demanded. Anchoring these attributes to the belt. Placing the pupil in the correct frame of mind.

He emerged from the cottage and trekked to the hill. Once there, he ascended, getting used to the new boots. The flexibleness and thinness of the soles provided little support.

As he approached, the structure loomed larger than he realized.

The green tiled ornate roof curved upward at the eaves with miniature sculpted lions protecting the Teahouse on each side. An emerald serpent spired from the middle and reached toward the heavens.

Red vertical beams held green wooden walls, with each section containing an octagonal window with a black diamond wrought-iron sill decorating the glass. Ironwork snaked around the entrance door, the walls, and roof, giving the appearance of clinging vines.

Vance lost his footing on the slippery grass. He glanced down at his feet instinctively as he steadied himself. When he looked back to the structure, he saw Kevin waiting for him on the railed walkway that circled the Teahouse.

Could Kevin have come outside so quickly without Vance seeing him? Vance waved and Kevin returned the gesture.

Kevin wore a black karate style uniform with tabi to match. His Japanese dogi, was the same as Vance's white traditional Korean dobak. The only difference was the color.

"Don't remove your boots," Kevin said. "It's not a *faux pas* to enter a dojo wearing tabi. We all wear them.

Vance nodded.

"Put on your black belt," Kevin said. "And we'll go inside."

Vance followed Kevin into the teahouse.

Twenty students worked techniques in pairs, their movements a mixture of linear jujutsu like strikes combined with circular Aikido style throws. As the students hit the ground, they broke their falls or rolled on tatami mats, making minimal noise.

Sho moved confidently through the fray toward them. Sho wore a gray business suit with black tabi. He made the combination look good.

"I thought you sheathed your sword?" Vance asked as Sho approached.

Sho bowed to them, and Vance and Kevin returned the gesture.

"Yes, for me and my family. They are not my blood."

"Why do you need me when you have such an accomplished group of students?"

"Not as skillful as you, Mr. Palladian," Sho said. "You have been tested in battle.

"Do you like it?" Sho asked, making a grand gesture. "The teahouse was built in the architectural style of the Song Dynasty."

"It's nice," Vance said, wondering why Sho was acting like a politician.

"Ah, you probably didn't notice that your client is here."

Vance followed Sho's pointer as it swept the room and stopped on a student. Vance blinked and the lovely convenience store girl came into focus.

She held her training partner off balance. She raised her head to look at them. Her eyes met his and then darted away. Her cheeks flushed. She returned to her opponent, kicking out his supporting leg, slamming him to the mats.

The hall fell quiet.

"Please, come here Jade," Sho said.

Jade left her partner on the floor and approached her dad.

The students returned to their practice.

Now it was Vance's turn to feel his cheeks burn. Her presence captivated him. Her hair, her eyes, her lips. The entire package—perfection.

"This is my daughter, Gyokko."

"I prefer Jade," she said. "Thank you for saving my life." She bowed to him. He bowed back.

"I thought you said you didn't teach family," Vance said, the words as dry as his throat.

"Jade is strong willed," Sho said. "Considering the attack, I knew she wouldn't be satisfied with only a bodyguard. If I didn't train her, she would have trained elsewhere."

Jade did her best to stifle a smile.

"I couldn't have that," Sho continued. "What they teach publicly was never meant for combat. The old ways have vanished, replaced with aesthetics and sports. That's why you ended up hospitalized. You didn't receive proper instruction."

Vance winced.

"You underestimate what's taught to the public," Vance said.

"Oh, do I? Do you feel well enough to attack an old man?"

What the hell was Sho's game?

Truthfully, he didn't feel one hundred percent, but he felt well enough, and angry enough, to tag an old guy, not hurt him, but tag him one.

"I guess I'm game if you are."

"That's what I like about you," Sho said. "Always up for a challenge."

Sho clapped his hands. The students stopped training. A phrase in Japanese and the group formed a circle around them. Jade and Kevin stepped back into the circle.

"Are you ready?" Sho asked. Vance knew he wasn't but nodded anyway.

"Good. Attack!"

Vance lifted his leg to execute a round kick, marveling at how easily his muscles remembered.

Rough hands from behind pushed him to the floor.

"You approach this like a sport. Last time you ended up dead to the world."

Vance forced himself up, feeling his muscles groan, and the damage to his pride. Kevin stood only a foot away behind him.

"How did he get so close silently" Vance asked, turning back to Sho.

The ring of students remained stone-faced, all except Jade. She giggled softly, mocking him.

Vance's anger flared. He took a deep breath, hoping to extinguish the fire.

"How indeed," Sho said. "That is a question you'll answer for yourself if you stay on. Like another shot? I promise this time, no tricks."

Vance didn't like the idea of Sho beating him up. He nodded anyway.

"Let's see if you can punch."

Vance fired a reverse punch at Sho's head.

Sho waited until the last second before floating outside the punch and disappearing into a blind spot. Now off balance, Vance felt cramping calf pain. Fell backward. Sho's thumbs pierced just below the TMJ, adding a terrible compression as Vance hit the tatami.

A thud as his head bounced off Sho's knee, the concussion echoing through his skull. He'd need more aspirin.

Sho clapped his hands, and the circle dispersed. Sho gave Vance a grin and nod before walking away to continue teaching.

Vance rolled into a squat. His whole body hurt.

Jade approached and tussled his hair. Her sardonic grin belied the longing in her eyes, a match to his own. Her eyes settled on Kevin, as she walked away.

When Sho finished teaching, he unceremoniously slipped outside. The students filed out in his wake, except for Kevin.

"So, what did you think?" Kevin asked.

"Impressive," Vance said, nodding his head.

"I'm glad you enjoyed it. Sho would like you to be his private student. It's a rare offer."

"I'm flattered," Vance said. "I figured after my performance today, he wouldn't be interested."

"You're interested?" Kevin asked, raising his eyebrows.

"I don't know what choice I have. But I'm reserving my judgment— for now," Vance said, looking down at his tabi. Then he looked Kevin in the eye. "How did you sneak up on me, anyway?"

"Sho would like to dine with you tonight. During dinner you can get all your questions answered."

Back at the cottage, Vance painted on deodorant and donned the outfit laid out for him. Black slacks, blue-collared shirt, gray sport coat, even the dress loafers fit perfectly.

He exited the cottage, wondering what the hike would do to his new shoes. Instead of a long walk, the stretch limo awaited him.

Kevin wore a black silk dress shirt sans tie, a black undershirt, revealed by the open collar, with slacks and loafers to match.

"What? You thought I'd make you walk to the mansion?" Kevin asked.

"Let's go, Jeeves," Vance said with a wink. He jumped into the passenger seat.

Kevin drove the limo up the winding hill toward the mansion. The night obscured much of the scenery. The limo's lights revealed trees and similar cottages that acted as a refuge for the live-in staff.

Kevin navigated into the turnaround, parking the limo in front of the mansion.

Vance exited the vehicle, not waiting for Kevin to open the door. He was unaccustomed to such niceties.

"I'll bring you in to see Sho," Kevin said, walking ahead of him.

The mansion looked as stately inside as the facade suggested. They entered a lavish foyer, lit brilliantly by a crystal chandelier. A grand staircase led to the upper level, all cast in marble, including the banister.

Vance followed Kevin through a hall adorned with Chinese and Japanese paintings. They passed through a wooden whitewashed door into a lavish dining room. A long table stood in the middle of the room. Three small chandeliers provided muted lighting appropriate for dining.

Sho stood.

"I'm glad you're having supper with me," Sho said, shaking Vance's hand. His grip strong for his age. "Thank you, Kevin."

Kevin nodded and turned to leave.

"Kevin won't be eating with us?" Vance asked.

"I have other plans, Mr. Palladian. But I appreciate you thinking of me," Kevin said. He turned and left the dining room.

"Kevin is a fine young man. He wouldn't find it stimulating to spend an evening with someone my age, or even your own."

"It's understandable."

"He's a little impetuous but will make a fine son-in-law," Sho said, gesturing for Vance to sit.

Vance's heart sank, and yet he couldn't understand why. Jade was too young for him. She needed someone closer to her own age.

Sho sat at the head of the table.

"Kevin and Jade are engaged, then?" Vance asked.

"Yes, and he's capable, but too close to make judgments about her safety."

As soon as they sat, a young Japanese woman wearing a black blazer, pants and female styled tie over a white ruffled blouse brought them a steaming bowl of clam chowder as their first course.

"I figured we'd start with something local," Sho said, unfolding his red cloth napkin onto his lap. He then reached for his soup spoon. Vance watched and copied him. He didn't want to seem uncouth.

The server returned with a bottle of chardonnay and poured them each half a glass.

"Please enjoy the food and the wine," Sho said. "The training will be harsh, and once you begin, the comforts few."

Vance didn't have to be told twice. He took a sip. The subtlety of the oak and smooth finish betrayed the exclusivity of the experience.

"I haven't decided if I want to stay on," Vance said, but that wasn't true. His will had already crumbled.

"Let me tell you something. It may solidify your resolve."

"I'm listening," Vance said.

"I'm going to be frank with you, Mr. Palladian. You saved my daughter, and I am forever in your debt. I will reward you handsomely."

"You've already done enough. I couldn't afford the medical bills."

"But," Sho continued, "I'm a very spiritual person. I practice a combination of Shinto, an indigenous religion, the original religion of the Japanese, and Mykko, an esoteric style of Buddhism, the Japanese equivalent to the Tibetan variety. What I'm getting at is that I had a vision."

"A vision? Like some sort of shamanic thing?"

"That's a good way to describe it. During a meditation, while you were in hospital, I saw you saving my daughter again. A second time. It's your destiny. I'm sure of it. So, I need you to stay on as her protector."

The salads arrived.

"I'm not sure if I believe in destiny or visions."

"Yes, I know. To modern sensibilities, they sound like superstitions or the ravings of a lunatic. But I have experienced too much not to heed what comes to me beyond my five natural senses. This sixth sense has saved many a warrior in ancient and modern times."

"Who wants to harm her?"

"I've become very successful in business. There are many who might want to harm us both."

Supper was served.

Vance feasted his eyes on a perfectly cooked filet mignon with a potato on the side. The meat was tender, juicy, and flavorful. The type of temptation that could make you forget all reservations. Still, after he finished chewing, he found the willpower to ask a long-standing question.

"What business are you in, Mr. Maramoto?" The wealth Sho surrounded himself with made Vance suspicious.

"The business of taking risks. The stock market, real estate. Sometimes I lose. Mostly I win. But then, you can see my success all around you."

"It's impressive," Vance said. "But you're holding something back."

"Good, Mr. Palladian!" Sho said, his voice rising. "Trusting your instincts is an important part of this training.

"I will level with you, even though I find it embarrassing. I have a son, Kudaki. When he was little, he was the son any father wishes for. As he got older, I realized he wasn't quite right. I ignored the warning signs, of course. He apprenticed with me and began his martial training. Unfortunately, when he went off to college, he had a mental breakdown. He became paranoid, but he was of age, and I didn't have control any longer."

"What happened?" Vance asked.

"He believed I was a villain, holding his sister Jade against her will, and made it his mission to destroy me and abduct Jade. Because of his mental issues he couldn't remain in college. He dropped out and began working for gangsters. He's ruthless, doesn't have a conscience. Attributes that allowed him to excel. Without my financial success, he would have overrun me."

"Isn't this a job for the police?"

"The police are corrupt in this state. It's all I can do to stay in their good graces. No, to protect Jade I have to rely on other means."

"You think he's going to kidnap her?"

"He's been planning it for years. Told me as much. He believes he's the reincarnation of a samurai, and that he has to stop us as his ancestors did in ancient times."

"Who's us?"

"I am a lineage holder. A soke. A grandmaster of the last remaining Shinobi ryu in existence."

"Shinobi?" Vance asked, shocked. "Are you saying…?"

"Yes. I head the last remaining school of Japan's ancient ninja assassins."

"So, you're a ninja?" Vance asked incredulously as Kevin drove down the winding road toward the cottage. "That's how you snuck up on me?"

"The ninja died out; we practice their martial traditions. It's rare to find a school that teaches the old ways. Most ryu, the schools, died off."

"How'd that happen?"

"They were no longer needed. After the Warring States Period, Japan found itself in an unprecedented time of peace," Kevin said. "We're really very lucky. Like Sho said, most martial arts today are taught as sports or character cultivation systems. The old warrior traditions have been lost."

Vance understood. Most of his former students didn't have or didn't care about the art's history. How it had come from China along the Silk Road into Okinawa, and used as a civilian defense art until the 1920's. Then it was introduced to Japanese school children as a way of building character and passing on the ancient warrior spirit that was no longer needed in the modern world.

During the brutal Japanese occupation of Korea, the Japanese executed the martial arts masters, later allowing only Koreans to study Japanese fighting systems.

After the occupation ended, the Korean government eventually unified the emancipated kwans (schools) under the moniker of Tae Kwon Do (translated as: Foot, Hand, Way). These kwans added the spirit of the ancient Korean martial sport of Taekkyon that focused on foot fighting. In that way Tae Kwon Do became known for its devastating kicks.

They didn't know, nor did they care, about the rough tutelage he suffered from his master teacher, Timothy Gold, a bare-knuckle, full contact karate fighter, who had learned the art while in the service and stationed in Korea. Those years of training had been brutal and militaristic.

He had had to run his school like a business, teaching children in order to fund the adult training. In a society that had become more and more litigious, he reduced the intensity of his classes. He longed for the old ways.

"I look forward to learning the old techniques," Vance said.

"It's more than that," Kevin said.

"What do you mean?"

"I can't tell you. I'll have to show you."

"When will that happen?"

"All in good time."

Kevin pulled the vehicle next to the cottage.

"Wear socks while you sleep," Kevin said.

"Why?"

"You know the Japanese don't ask questions. They obey," Kevin said, then smiled.

Vance laughed.

"I'm not Japanese."

"Nobody's perfect," Kevin said with a wink. "The socks will keep your feet warm. Chinese medicine. Cold feet make it hard to fall into a deep sleep. And you're going to need your sleep."

Vance couldn't argue with that logic.

"See you in the morning," Kevin said.

Vance shut the limo door and Kevin pulled away. Then the limo stopped, white lights as the vehicle reversed its direction.

"I almost forgot," Kevin said. "Before bed, find the stone padlocks I made you. You'll need them for tomorrow."

"Stone padlock…?" Vance began, but Kevin pulled away, driving back toward the gate leading to the world Vance had left behind.

Chapter Four

"Wake up, sleepyhead."

Vance jerked awake, eyes wide, breathing labored, body in fight or flight. He sat up, arms raised, fists clenched, ready for offense.

A man stood in the half-light of the cottage.

He had wings!

Vance blinked to dispel the illusion.

Only Kevin.

"How d'you get in here?" Vance asked. He'd locked the door before bed. At least he thought so. Then he remembered the staff had keys to the cabin. Most likely, Kevin did as well.

"I'm a ninja," Kevin said with a wink. "Remember?"

"Real funny." Vance said. "What time is it?"

"Early enough to catch the worm," Kevin said.

Vance blinked sleep from his eyes. The alarm clock on the nightstand read *5:30 a.m.*

"You find those stone padlocks?" Kevin asked.

"Yeah, they're right over there," Vance said, pointing to the corner of the room. They looked like square kettle bells with wooden handles.

"Good. Get dressed; wear outdoor training clothes. Bring the padlocks with you."

"What about breakfast?" Vance asked.

"Train first, eat later," Kevin said with a wink.

"Great," Vance said, his stomach rumbling. Not even time for a morning shit.

Vance rummaged through the dresser, grabbing a pair of black workout pants, a sweat wicking shirt, and a zip-up hoody sweatshirt.

What the hell was this thing? A magic wardrobe?

Every time he opened it, he found the exact clothing needed.

"Are we meeting Sho?"

"You'll see," Kevin said. "Are we going to talk or get dressed."

After he finished changing, Kevin led him outside into the crisp morning air. A deep breath revitalized him, made him feel almost alive. Much better than the stale air in the hospital room.

Kevin wore a black tracksuit that emphasized his broad shoulders, making him look more imposing than before.

"We're going for a run," Kevin said.

"Am I up for a run?" Vance asked, mostly to himself. After so long in a coma, he had lost confidence in his conditioning.

"Only one way to find out," Kevin answered as if the question weren't rhetorical.

Vance and Kevin walked side by side on the asphalt road until veering onto a well-worn trail surrounded by trees. Vance felt relieved, he didn't think his knees could take the pounding on hard ground. As they continued, the pathway became steep, and Vance's breathing labored. The stone padlocks weighed him down.

"Roll your feet, heel to edge until your foot touches the ground, then repeat with the other foot. Bend your knees. Very good. Keep your arms straight, don't pump them. If your arms drift with the weight of the padlocks, you're doing it wrong."

When the trail leveled out, they broke into a light run.

"Always keep one foot on the ground for stability."

This new way of moving felt awkward, yet surprisingly efficient. Vance kept his center of gravity low and abstained from upper body movement, head remaining on the same vertical plain just like performing old school Tae Kwon Do punches and blocks.

"Why are we running like this?" Vance asked, unable to contain his Western curiosity.

"In ancient times, Shinobi needed to run long distances while still maintaining the energy to fight when they reached their destination.

They also had to move quietly. They were well versed in *mu on no ho*, ninja silent running."

"Sounds romantic," Vance mused.

"Romantic? Romance should be the furthest thing from your mind," Kevin said with a sly grin. But a darkness flittered behind his eyes.

"What are you talking about?" Vance asked. But he knew. A cold sweat erupted at his hairline.

"You're kidding, right? I saw the way you looked at Jade," Kevin said.

"You don't have to worry about me. I'm much too old for her."

"I'm not worried. Sho's the one you'd have to worry about."

"Sho's in his seventies," Vance said and then remembered his encounter and laughed. "Yeah, I see your point."

"In our tradition, age only makes us spiritually stronger," Kevin said.

Vance nodded instead of speaking—already winded.

"Breathe in rhythm with your movement. Inhale and exhale with each step. Your breath should be like a baby, and your face should reflect the stillness of an undisturbed pond. By synchronizing your breathing and releasing exertion, you'll find you're able to train longer and harder."

Vance followed Kevin's instructions. In short order, his breathing slowed, and his heart returned to a safe rhythm. He had the feeling, perhaps the illusion, that he could continue running indefinitely.

When the pathway grew steep, they bent forward and walked up the incline. On the downgrade they sidewinded to reduce muscle resistance. The efficiency of movement wasn't lost on Vance. He didn't think he could have kept up without it.

When the footpath ended, they emerged onto a well-manicured hill behind the property overlooking the shimmering waters of Narraganset Bay.

Slick with sweat, Vance marveled at how quickly his breathing normalized.

"While holding the stone padlocks, practice your punches, strikes, and blocks. Unify your movements with the waves in the bay. We call this *sui no kata kokyu ho*, water exercise."

Vance did as instructed until awkwardness and frustration overtook him. Trying to match the rhythm of the water while straining against the weights corrupted his muscle memory.

"You're trying too hard," Kevin said. "Just let go."

Vance's arms burned from the stone's added weight. Slowly he merged with the ocean, with its rhythms and cycles. A oneness he had never known before. Discomfort faded. He became the waves, sucked in, and spit out, crashing like a breaker over the rocks. As soon as he discovered his rhythm, Kevin stopped him.

"That's enough moving meditation for today," Kevin said.

But it wasn't. He had found peace, a stillness elusive even with Zen practice. He wanted to merge with the ocean, plunge back into watery bliss.

"I don't want you to think of the blocks you just performed as blocks," Kevin said.

"How do you want me to think of them?" Vance asked, wishing he could go back to the Zen like exercise he had practiced previously.

"Sho calls them *Happo Biken*, eight secret swords. They are the foundation of how Sho will remake you as a martial artist."

"What do you mean?" Vance asked.

"How often have you utilized a down block in sparring?" Kevin asked.

"Probably never," Vance said.

"So, why do you practice them?" Kevin asked, raising an eyebrow.

"Tradition? They're part of the curriculum? I was afraid not to pass them down. I figured if the masters put it in the art, they had a reason."

"They did indeed. Let me give you an example," Kevin said. "Please throw a thrusting front kick at me."

Vance stepped back with his right leg. He rolled his foot, creating a springing momentum while lifting his knee and letting his foot thrust forward. Pushing out his right hip while pulling back with his left shoulder, creating an antagonistic movement to generate maximum power.

Kevin moved back diagonally, offline from the attack, at the same time executing a down block. His knuckles connected with the inside of Vance's knee joint. Pain exploded at the point of contact, numbing Vance's upper and lower leg, and sending his trajectory in the opposite direction.

Vance gritted his teeth as his tabi covered foot touched the ground and buckled. He found himself staring up from the ground, holding his throbbing knee.

"Don't worry," Kevin said. "You haven't been damaged permanently."

"That's comforting," Vance said as he gingerly returned to his feet. His leg held his weight and the throbbing lessened. A nice bruise would develop later.

"I'll reset the nerve," Kevin said. He squatted down, slapped the affected area twice and then rubbed in a clockwise motion. Vance felt better.

"Now I want you to hit me with a vertical fist," Kevin said as he moved back to his original starting point. "I'm going to show you how to use the outside block."

Reluctantly, Vance did as he was told. He threw the punch and Kevin attacked his arm the same as his leg, batting it out of the way, an explosion of pain and numbness radiating out from his elbow. Automatically, without thought, Vance followed up with a traditional reverse punch. Kevin easily slipped outside, this time his strike arching up to find the *kyusho* pain point hidden underneath Vance's arm.

"You really like beating me up, don't you?" Vance said as he tried to shake the feeling back into his arms, the ache maddening.

"I've put the teeth back into your martial art," Kevin said as he reset the nerves. "I want you to think of cutting with your blocks as if you held an invisible sword, a secret sword. Now throw one more thrusting front kick, I promise I won't hurt your leg this time."

Kevin's assurances didn't comfort him.

Despite his reservations, Vance launched a kick. This time Kevin moved diagonally to the outside of Vance's kicking leg and made a semi-circular movement with his extended arm, catching Vance's leg, and then dumping him hard onto his back.

Vance gasped for breath, realizing he should have slapped the ground to dissipate the impact, like a judoka, or at least breathed out harshly, the way boxers received a body blow. Instead, he sucked wind.

"Linear lines are for striking. Circular lines are for knocking off balance and throwing. If we were on a battlefield in ancient Japan, I would have sent you down onto your pelvis and shattered it. Once helpless, you'd be easy to kill."

More comforting thoughts.

"I guess I've battered you enough," Kevin said. "In our cool down I'll give you the first secret of the ninja's silent movement skills."

Kevin had Vance sit down and rotate all his joints in a circle starting with his toes, moving up to his ankles. Then Vance stood and repeated the movement with his knees, his hips, his shoulders, and finally his head.

"Circular rotation is good for your body and your internal energy systems, but the ninja did these exercises to lessen the popping and cracking of their joints. The absence of these noises aids in silent movement."

"How did you find our training session?" Kevin asked as they made their way back down the trail.

"Enlightening," Vance said, and he only meant it slightly sarcastically. Despite the pain he still felt, Vance knew he had been introduced to a different philosophy of fighting. His earlier training had been constrained by rules. Kevin had shown him what lay beyond convention.

"Have a good breakfast," Kevin said once they had returned to the cottage. "You won't be seeing Sho until later tonight. He wants to work with you privately. I have to find out what he would like you to do for the rest of the day."

Kevin jumped in the limo and headed to parts unknown.

Famished, Vance entered the cottage and went straight for the kitchen. A moment of indecision and then he felt inspired. He pulled a cast iron skillet out of a cabinet, and then three eggs, cheese, mushrooms, and ham from the fully stocked refrigerator.

A few minutes later he had an omelet with burnt wheat toast, just the way he liked it, slathered with a raspberry fruit spread.

Vance sat down at the small table with his food and a cup of black percolated coffee and went at his breakfast greedily, wondering what Kevin and Sho would have in store for him next.

Not long after Vance finished breakfast, Kevin returned.

"Here's the deal," Kevin said. "Sho wants you to meet up with the landscapers and give them a hand."

"I'm working for my supper?" Vance asked. He tried to hide his irritation. He should be grateful for the activity, but being asked to tend to the grounds felt so devoid of anything he was training for. He really couldn't see the point. He didn't think Sho needed free labor.

"I think this assignment will surprise you. When you find the crew, ask for Jax," Kevin said. Vance shrugged his shoulders and tried to push away the annoyance that had washed over him.

When Vance met up with the grounds crew they were already well into their workday. He made a beeline for a big man who matched the description Kevin had given him.

The foreman was a big framed Asian with unfashionably long hair and looked more Samoan than Japanese. He wore work boots, heavy military style pants, and a blue long-sleeve work shirt. His biceps and triceps bulged through the material, as if he wrestled with iron all day, every day. He stood, his back to Vance, looking like an overseer, the master of all he surveyed.

"Jax?" Vance asked as he came into earshot.

The big man turned around to reveal a countenance equally imposing.

"Vance?" Jax said in a deep baritone, and then held out his meaty hand. "Kevin said you'd be arriving."

As he shook it, Vance marveled at this man's control. He had expected to have his bones crushed. Instead, Jax's grip belied the true strength the man possessed.

"They want to put me to work," Vance said, and smiled. He didn't feel much like smiling.

"They want to teach you how to hide in plain sight," Jax said. "Estate gardening will be your introduction to the *shinobi onshinjutsu*, invisibility training."

"So, these men are ninja?" Vance asked, moving his hand in a wide slow arc to include all the workers. They drove riding lawnmowers or whacked weeds. The sweet tang of fresh mowed grass scented the air.

"No. These men are criminals. They're prisoners on work furloughs. You don't want to let your guard down around these men."

"Good to know," Vance said. He wanted to ask why they were repaying their debt to society by providing free labor to Sho but decided against it. He didn't have to be told about the politics of the world or the perks that could be gained by someone able to game the system.

Jax grabbed a weed-whacker from the back of a small trailer attached to a riding mower and handed it to Vance.

Vance headed toward the manor home and began his work as far away from the others as possible. He pulled the ripcord and the machine sputtered to life, assailing him with a deafening hum and a maddening vibration as he lopped off anything that he noticed sprouting where it didn't belong.

As the sun heated the day, he stopped the machine, removed his shirt, and wiped the sweat from his brow and his chest. Back when he ran the martial arts school, Vance had had to pick up some extra work, but he never performed manual labor. The most exercise he received from his side-hustle was a light jaunt around a building doing rounds in a security uniform.

His thoughts were interrupted as a strange feeling overcame him, the hairs prickling on the back of his neck. He turned and looked up. Someone in the window above him moved quickly out of sight. Who had been watching him? Jade? He liked the thought.

"Where're you doing your time, man?"

Startled, Vance spun around. A prisoner stood before him; his orange pants screamed Property of Rhode Island Department of Corrections, and his torso and arms wore a scrawling ink work that had become ubiquitous in the youth and MMA cultures, but at one time had marked the wearer as having done hard time. The man's scarred and pocked face reflected the tough unforgiving life he had led.

"I didn't," Vance said, and immediately regretted it.

"Let's just get something straight. You think you work for Jax? You don't. You work for me. Unless you want to be fertilizer for the garden."

The man skulked away from Vance, and the relative shade of the building, into the unrelenting sunlight.

"Who's that?" Vance asked Jax, returning to grab a mower. Vance subtly nodded his head toward the man in question.

"That's Slade," Jax said. "Watch out for him. He's in prison for life. He don't care who he kills."

"And they let him out on work furlough?"

"Bring it up with the state," Jax said. "He threaten you?"

"You could say that," Vance said.

"I can talk to Sho," Jax said. "Find something else for you to do."

"No. I'll tough it out," Vance said. He was tempted to take Jax up on the offer, but he didn't want to run at the first sign of trouble.

Jax looked deep in thought for a moment.

"Let's go to the house," Jax said. "I have things to show you."

Jax brought Vance into a small room in the basement of the building. The accommodations were sparse. Assorted dumbbells rested against the far wall; a heavy bag hung in the corner of the room. A single naked bulb lit the whole scene.

"This is my private dojo," Jax said. "I like to train in the woods like my ancestors, but there is a time and a place for a gym like this."

"Why did you bring me here?" Vance asked. He didn't think Jax was one for show and tell.

"The ninjutsu that Sho is teaching you, the ancient techniques are sound. Even Korean Karate can be formidable when trained correctly. But you should know how to deal with modern threats. If Slade attacks you, he'll be using a prison fighting system known as the Cell Block Shuffle."

"Cute name," Vance said and then laughed through his nose. What the hell was he getting himself into?

"It's a combination of dirty boxing, submission wresting, and prison shank fighting passed down from one felon to the next."

Jax sounded like he had some experience surviving behind bars, but Vance wasn't about to ask him.

"You ever done any boxing?" Jax asked.

"I know the basic punches," Vance said. It wasn't unusual for Korean masters to add boxing to their repertoire, making their hands as dangerous as their feet.

"That's a good start," Jax said. "We'll build from there."

Jax wrapped Vance's hands and wrists to protect them from blunt force trauma. Then he helped Vance into a pair of bag gloves.

Loosening up, Vance shadowboxed, various combinations of the basics, staying mobile. Jab. Cross. Hook. Uppercut.

Jax demonstrated twisting his feet and hips to add power to the punches, and Vance mimicked his form.

Feeling more confident, Vance let loose on the heavy bag in a close approximation of Western style kickboxing.

Once he had worked up a good sweat Jax stopped him.

"Now I'll show you the illegal moves that will keep you on top," Jax said.

Jax showed him how to hit the bicep to destroy the limb, how to add elbows, and gouge the eyes. He taught him to step on his opponent's foot to knock him to the ground, where to hit the hip to hobble the other fighter while protecting the fist from damage, and a host of other nasty tricks.

After Jax finished the lesson, Vance felt more formidable, his confidence increased.

"We'll get back to work," Jax said. "Tomorrow, I have something else to show you."

Vance finished his workday without further incident. He tried to keep to himself and stay invisible. He figured it's what a shinobi would do.

The work had kept his body busy, and his mind rested on the martial techniques Jax had showed him. They were harsh, ruthless, and exactly what he'd need if Slade attacked him.

Chapter Five

Detective Christian Keikan awoke, as he always did, a few minutes before 6:00 a.m., seconds ahead of the alarm. Grabbing his smart phone off the nightstand, he swiped at the screen, canceling it.

His jaw was tight with worry. Having tossed and turned all night, he'd drag ass for the rest of the day.

The cramped apartment acted as a financial penance. Eventually, he'd have a nice cushion. Then he could settle down and raise a family.

Butterflies erupted at the thought. Would the curse that raged through his family destroy his progeny?

He didn't want to think about curses or his family. Instead, he crawled out of bed and got down on bended knee. He placed his palms together in what the Japanese called *gasho* and prayed.

This simple act of supplication quieted his mind and filled him with confidence that would pull him through the day.

After a hurried shower, he made quick work of a bowl of oatmeal and a banana protein shake. Filled with carbs and whey, he stepped into black slacks, slipped into a gray sport coat, and headed for the parking garage.

He tried to quiet his mind as he navigated his Mazda 6 through the streets of Providence, Rhode Island.

After earning a bachelor's degree in criminal justice, he had quickly acquired a job on the beat in the Providence department. His Japanese ethnicity assisted him in navigating the Asian community and helped him to rise in the ranks and reach detective.

The wheels and cogs in the machinery of life had moved so smoothly, he couldn't help but think destiny had somehow intervened, or that his own mission had been ordained by divine providence.

He swung into Dunkin' Donuts and grabbed a coffee with extra milk and sugar just by saying, "Extra, extra." The words always made him think of a 1940s newspaper barker.

Discipline defined his life, but he allowed for a few indulgences. Besides, the caffeine would make him feel better. Many native New Englanders enjoyed iced coffee all year long, even in the dead of winter. That wasn't for Keikan, and neither was coffee milk, a staple culinary delight in Rhode Island. But then, he hadn't been born in America's smallest state and hadn't acquired a taste for the things Rhode Islanders loved.

Keikan turned onto Atwells Avenue, driving under the gateway arch, with its bronze La Pigna, and onto Federal Hill. As a child, he had thought the weathered copper-green pinecone, suspended from the top of the structure, was a pineapple. He still thought it looked like a pineapple. Four miniature Greek columns held the arch aloft.

Every time he passed under the La Pigna, he felt symbolically renewed.

The pinecone itself was a traditional Italian symbol of welcome, abundance, and quality, and reminded Keikan of the 1st century Fontana Della Pigna that had once stood near the Pantheon adjacent to the Temple of Isis, but now resided in a wall niche at the Vatican.

He continued past Italian restaurants, most closed until noon, and assorted convenience stores, sandwich shops, and pizza parlors. Commuters hustled down sidewalks with morning coffees and newspapers toward their offices or cars to greet a new workday.

Keikan turned onto Washington Street, where the Providence Public Safety Complex awaited him. The structure, a multi-faced building, held the Municipal Court, Fire Department, and Police Department.

The sun glinted off glass, obscuring the atrium that extended like a wedge in front of the concrete building.

Keikan parked in a reserved spot in the garage, and then hurried across the street, entering the complex through the atrium.

Having been built in 2002, the interior kept a sterile modern aesthetic that felt corporate despite the blue-collar nature of emergency services.

The chief looked up from his work as Keikan entered the department's main floor, filled with low walled cubicles manned by both uniformed and plain-clothed officers.

Police Chief Hunter Clemens noticed him right away and motioned with two fingers for Keikan to come hither.

The chief's office reminded him of Sleeping Beauty's glass coffin. For some reason, it unnerved him.

This is what he had been fretting over all night. Might as well get it over with.

No time like the present. He snatched two folders from his desk and headed over to face the music.

"Have a seat," Clemens said. He was in his mid-fifties but didn't look a day over sixty-five. He wore a white dress shirt with a loosened tie that looked like an upside-down noose. The chief tossed his reading glasses on his messy desk and rubbed the bridge of his bulbous nose as if trying to stave off a sinus headache.

Keikan sat in an adjacent chair, folders covering his lap. The chair was unsteady, as if one leg was too short.

Attached to the glass walls by Velcro hung diplomas from various colleges: a Bachelor of Arts Degree in Business from the University of Rhode Island, a Bachelor of Science in the Administration of Justice from Roger Williams College, the same as Keikan, and a Master's in Criminal Justice from Boston College. If nothing else, the chief valued education.

"I'm getting a lot of calls about you," Clemens said. Now he rubbed his forehead as if talking to Keikan gave him a headache.

"From who?"

"From who? Who do you think? Well, they're not coming from him, if that's what you're thinking. They're coming from people high up politically. You appreciate how the system works, don't you?"

"I'm slowly gathering evidence…."

"Listen Chris, you're too close to this. I realize you've got a lot of skin in the game, but you're going to get busted down to desk-work. I won't have any choice. I don't want to see that. You're too valuable an asset to the department, not to mention our diversity quotas."

The chief laughed through his nose before continuing.

"Know what I mean? You're bright. Pick up shit quick. That's important. Your job is to assist vice and homicide, not to stake out everyone who works for the Maramoto organization."

"They're an organized crime family," Keikan said, growing frustrated.

"We have a bunch of crime families in this city, a lot of criminals. Most of them are politicians. Now, I'm going to give you a new assignment."

Keikan shifted uncomfortably in his chair.

A young female cop in duty blues, her blonde hair tied back, opened the door after a brief knock. She stuck her head in only part way as if she worried the chief might throw something at her. Keikan wouldn't put it past him.

"The commissioner is on line one."

The chief grunted and shook his head. Keikan stood. Time to make a break for it. Clemens was a busy guy. If he left now it might be a few weeks before the chief would remember to reassign him.

Clemens motioned for Keikan to sit. Keikan slumped into the chair.

"Commissioner, what can I do for you?" The chief's voice sounded cheery, but his expression remained sour. "Yeah, I know who he is. Yeah, yeah, I can find a place for him out of the way. No problem. Okay great, talk to you later."

Clemens hung up, looked at Keikan and chuckled. This couldn't be good.

"The Man Upstairs is smiling down at you, Keikan," Clemens said in his best Irish accent. "You want your wild goose chase? Fine. Two conditions."

"Go on," Keikan said, holding his breath.

"Fly under the radar. Collect intelligence. Do stakeouts, write reports, reports that will come directly to me. And do not, I repeat, do not engage."

"What if someone lets me on the property?"

"In that case, I have no problem with it. Of course, you'd have to convince Newport P.D. to assist you. Good luck with that on both counts. Just no more phone calls."

"What's the other condition?"

"I'm assigning you a new partner. His name is George Hayden."

"The crazy guy who writes the true crime books?" Keikan asked.

"That's him. And yes, he's crazy as a loon. But no matter how much trouble he causes, the police union won't let me fire him. He'll be retiring soon. The commissioner wants him somewhere out of sight. You know, a dead end.

"If you babysit him, you'll have a small window to bust Maramoto's ass. But if you mess this up, I'll bust you down to Desk Sergeant. You can do intake and answer phones for the rest of your career. Maybe traffic duty during the winter. Who knows? Just understand, I'll make your life hell. We have a deal?"

"Deal," Keikan said. He already regretted it.

Keikan snaked through the halls and corridors of the complex, his footfalls echoing in the expanse, passing by the sunlit windows that cast triangles of light on the marbled floor. He turned and descended a stairway, gliding his hand over a cool iron handrail into the bowels of the building.

The cramped area filled with rows of battered desks had been dubbed, very unoriginally, the dungeon, and Keikan had been told that this was where the undesirables within the force ended up.

Clemens had told Keikan, more than once, and only half-kiddingly, that he'd one day end up here, and when he did, he would eventually long for traffic duty as his skin became pasty, and his eyes grew dim with disuse, until he would never be able to emerge into the sunlight again. To look at the place and the denizens who inhabited it, Keikan figured it wasn't hyperbole.

George Hayden sat hunched over a pile of papers, trying his best to look busy. He had a round face, an out-of-date mustache, a balding dome, and wore an older style tweed jacket that smelled of mothballs.

Keikan recognized Hayden from his author photo. He couldn't remember which one he had read. He had bought the book one day before jumping on a plane and heading to a conference in Portland, Oregon. Instead of reading, he'd fallen asleep and never picked it up again. Although, he had always meant to. He should bring it in and have the old buzzard sign the thing. Might be worth something after Hayden had been put out to pasture or died. Death wasn't unusual after retirement. The last he had heard, statistics gave men three years.

"Hayden?" Keikan asked. Hayden didn't react. The old bastard must be deaf.

Great.

Keikan was just about to speak louder when Hayden blinked, sat up, and turned to him.

"So, you're my new partner," Hayden said, his eyes droopy.

"You look thrilled," Keikan said.

"I would be, if you were anything but a babysitter," Hayden said, giving a weak smile. "How'd you get such an illustrious assignment?"

"Went after a mob boss with connections. The Chief planned to take me off the case. Then the Commissioner called about you."

"And he'll let you work in the background if you keep me out of trouble," Hayden said.

"That's what he told me."

"Figures. Whatever keeps the Commissioner happy." Hayden motioned to the seat next to him in front of an equally battered desk.

"Thought we'd go someplace a little sunnier," Keikan said.

"What's your name?" Hayden said, ignoring him.

"Christian, Chris Keikan."

"Okay, Chris. Have a seat. Let's talk for a minute."

Against his better judgment, he did as Hayden asked. There was something about Hayden. Perhaps his age made him appear grandfatherly, made Keikan want to follow his direction.

Still, he felt, if he sat down, he wouldn't be moving from the bowels of the building for a long time, maybe, like the Chief had told him, he'd never get out. He sat anyway.

"You have to understand that if you want to do things under the radar you have to go where no one will be looking for you, where no one will observe what you're doing and start questioning you. You must give up all hopes of promotion and work at the task at hand until you get your outcome. If you can do that, you'll be able to scratch the itch that's driving you mad, and you might even get your goal before they find out and shut you down.

"You know, I see a little of myself in you. The young me. You want to take down this guy really bad, I can tell by the look in your eyes. It's an obsession. The question is: why? What's driving you, Chris?"

Keikan didn't answer, but he didn't break eye contact either. What Hayden wanted to know was none of his business.

"Okay, you don't have to tell me," Hayden said. "I'll find out eventually anyway. Well, since you're the man in charge, what do you want to do first?"

"Why don't I show you the lay of the land?" Keikan said. "You up for a drive to Newport?"

"Newport?" Hayden looked exasperated. "Over the bridge?"

What was it about native Rhode Islanders? They never wanted to drive over that damn bridge. They never wanted to drive anywhere. If Paul Revere had been a Rhode Islander, he never would have taken his midnight ride, and the American Revolutionary War would have been lost.

"Unless you want to go by boat," Keikan said.

"Okay," Hayden said. "But I'm driving."

Keikan followed Hayden to the parking lot on the east side. Reserved for patrol cars and a few unmarked cruisers. They approached a faded dark blue early-model Crown Victoria.

"You've got to be kidding," Keikan said.

"It's a good year," Hayden said as he fumbled with his key ring. He finally found the right one and slipped it into the lock. Keikan missed using an electronic key fob already.

The vehicle looked as old inside as it did outside, but at least Hayden had meticulously vacuumed the interior and all the plastic glistened with Armor-All.

Keikan bent down in front of the Vic.

"What the hell are you doing?" Hayden asked.

"Just removing the front plate," Keikan said. "Don't worry. I'll put it back on when we get back."

They shot out onto the street. Keikan smiled despite himself. At least Hayden didn't drive like an old man.

"Family?" Hayden asked.

Keikan's stomach flip-flopped.

"Huh?" Keikan asked, stalling, hoping to drop the subject.

"Have any kids?" Hayden asked.

"No children," Keikan said with a sigh. "Not even married, yet."

"It will happen in time. Drive your demons from your system before you pursue a family. Hard enough staying out of divorce court as a cop."

Keikan sensed Hayden had something he wanted to get off his chest, something he was reluctant to reveal. Keikan didn't really care to hear Hayden's tales of woe, but prodding Hayden, allowing him to talk, would keep him from exhuming skeletons better left unearthed.

"I'm sure you know all about it," Keikan said.

"You bet I do," Hayden said. "I had this one case where I was sure, this one bastard did it. He removed the eyes of exotic dancers after he killed them, replaced their eyes with glass replicas scrawled with runes and magical symbols. Gruesome stuff. He thought they were witches trying to open the gates to hell, some crazy shit like that."

"But he got away with it?" Keikan prompted. He could almost see the wheels turning in Hayden's brain as he remembered the most baffling and obsession-riddled case of his life.

"Yeah, we could never prove he did anything. A lot got suppressed in court. I brought the evidence out in a book."

"That how you got started writing?"

"Oh, I'm no writer. I have a guy ghost it for me. I sit and tell him stories; he records the sessions, types them up later. Makes everything connect. It's almost like going to a psychiatrist except authors can't write you a prescription."

Hayden laughed ruefully at that, and Keikan wondered how many psychotropic drugs Hayden had been on during his career.

Cops tended to self-medicate at the nearest watering holes, but sometimes they liked to mix booze with pills to help them forget the sick and twisted things they witnessed day in and day out.

Keikan couldn't blame the ones who had succumbed to addiction but was determined not to let it happen to him.

"Anyway, I decided the best way forward was to get the information out to the public. Maybe someone would notice a slip up if he started killing again. Eventually a publishing company gave me a contract and that's how my writing career started.

"After the book came out the perp sued me and the publisher for defamation. We settled out of court with the publisher scrubbing his name from all new editions. He still got damages from me, and I came close to financial ruin.

"Those books made me somewhat infamous, but they continued to sell well, and eventually got me out of debt. Even helped me pay for my daughter's tuition. We had a kid late in life. A miracle really. My daughter was traumatized in school by my notoriety. We're pretty much estranged."

"Wow! That's heavy shit," Keikan said. And he meant it. This guy was carrying around serious baggage. Maybe Hayden wasn't as insane as everyone thought. Maybe his crazy theories were only the embellishments of a ghostwriter's overactive imagination blending Hayden's real-life experiences with creative fiction. Keikan guessed only time would tell.

"The moral here, Chris, is you don't want to follow down my path. Do what you need to do. Get your shit handled and then get on with your life. Like I say, you don't want to plague your children with your demons."

Keikan knew all too much about demons, some of them tore away invisibly at your soul, the guilt of things left undone, words left unsaid. But there were real demons in the world. Had seen them with his own eyes. He could tell that Hayden had met them too, had battled them, almost losing his family, his soul, perhaps his very life.

"There's always that one case. It will destroy you if you let it. Don't let it!"

"Ready to shake things up?" Keikan asked once they'd crossed the Newport Bridge.

"What do you have in mind?" Hayden asked, wearily.

"Apply pressure," Keikan said. "Then secure backup."

"Something tells me, I'm not going to like this," Hayden said shaking his head.

A few miles down the road, Keikan pointed, "There it is. Let's go take a look."

"Take a look?" Hayden asked, slowing to make the turn. "Thought we were going under the radar."

"Trust me," Keikan said. "We're not going to do anything illegal."

Reluctantly, Hayden turned onto the access road. The road was flanked on either side by a rock wall that held back the encroaching woods.

Keikan's fingers twitched with adrenaline. He placed his palm on his forehead, keeping his elbow down.

"You got a headache?" Hayden asked.

"No," Keikan said. "I'm hiding my face."

"Oh yeah," Hayden said. "That'll work."

"It will work for the security camera. That's why I removed the plate, " Keikan said. "Here's what you need to do..."

Keikan gave Hayden instructions.

"I have enough trouble with computers," Hayden said. "You want me to use your smartphone?"

The light had gradually faded as the sun neared the last leg of its descent. But there was still sufficient illumination for what needed doing.

Hayden slowed to a stop in front of the gate, then exited the vehicle.

Keeping his eyes on Hayden, Keikan hunkered down, further obscuring his features. If the chief received another phone call....

"I'm looking for directions to Steadman Street," Hayden said to the approaching guard. The gate's bars separated them.

"This is private property," the uniformed Japanese sentry said. Keikan didn't recognize him.

"I'm not going onto the estate" Hayden said, feigning exasperation, holding up the smart phone. "The GPS whatever on this thing keeps leading me in circles."

"If you don't leave, I'll call the police," the guard said, voice and posture becoming more authoritative.

"Thanks for nothing," Hayden said, returning to his vehicle, backing down the road so the guard couldn't record the license plate.

"You get his picture?" Keikan asked.

"I did. That was easy," Hayden said, handing off the smartphone to Keikan. "Guess you can teach an old dog new tricks."

"This is a wonderful first date, Chris," Officer Stacy Pepper said, taking a sip of decaf coffee. "I'm surprised you didn't bring your chaperone."

"Hayden?" Keikan peaked out the donut shop window. Hayden reclined in the driver's seat; eyes already closed. "More like the other way around."

Stacy liked him. It was obvious. Sure, he was attracted. She was a real looker, especially for a cop, and a Mixed Martial Arts fighter to boot.

He liked her long blond hair, even braided into a ponytail and hidden under her uniform collar. A uniform that hugged and accentuated her curves, salvaged her femininity, a side he'd enjoy exploring in the future.

Police work and martial arts provided common interests. She fought amateur MMA matches under the name Stacy "Hot Sauce" Pepper. If she hadn't transferred to Newport PD, they'd have hooked up. Currently, the time wasn't right for a relationship.

"What type of favor?" Stacy asked with a wink.

"I've got the go-ahead for the Maramoto Estate," Keikan said.

"Really?" Stacy asked, raising her eyebrows. Clearly not buying it. "The chief's letting you make an arrest outside your jurisdiction?"

"That's what I need you for," Keikan said. He regretted the phrasing. He didn't want her to think he was using her, even if that's exactly what he was doing.

"What do I tell *my* chief?" Stacy asked.

"Nothing," Keikan said. "Once on the estate, I'll request backup. Invite you onto the property. Could be a big deal if we bust this guy."

He bit his lip. She pursed hers, mulling it over.

Come on, come on….

"Okay, I'll do it," she said. "But under one condition."

"I'm not going to like it. Am I?"

"Aw, it's not so bad. I hope," Stacy said, and then smiled. "You make this arrest; you have to take me on a real date. No coffee shops or roadside diners."

Keikan feigned a look of deep thought. She playfully slapped his arm.

"Okay, okay," he said, grinning. A rare occurrence. His face returned to stone. "You've got your date. Name the place. But not until we've busted this guy. Agreed?"

She nodded.

Keikan stood, bent over, and gave her a gentle peck on the cheek, inhaling the subtle scent of lilacs and lavender.

A startled yet cheerful expression colored her face. He threw her a wink, then turned to leave.

"Bye, Keikan," she said teasingly. He didn't turn around, just kept walking.

He felt bad. She didn't know what she was getting into.

Chapter Six

The long first day had ended and Vance trudged wearily down the hill toward the cottage. He hoped for food and a little sleep, but it looked like Kevin had a different plan. Kevin leaned against the limo, arms folded.

"There's more?" Vance asked.

"It's been a long day," Kevin said. "But there are people you should meet. Why don't you take a fast shower, make a quick sandwich, and I'll have you back before you turn into a pumpkin."

Vance nodded and went inside. He reemerged twenty minutes later, freshly hosed off and wearing a polo shirt and khakis, his stomach satisfied on shaved roast beef.

Slipping into the passenger seat, Kevin sped off before Vance could secure his seatbelt.

An hour later, they arrived at a nondescript brick building in Providence, pulled into a small alley that now acted as off-street parking, and then exited the vehicle. A breeze rustled Vance's shirt. The cool night wind exhilarated him, made him feel alive.

Kevin pulled out a key ring and unlocked a battered metal door. The foyer had trapped the odor of fifty years' worth of inhabitants.

He followed Kevin down a set of worn, carpeted stairs into a dingy and uninviting hallway. The keys jangling. Kevin unlocked the door, and they entered.

"Wow. Nice digs," Vance said, truly impressed. The exterior gave the impression of squalor with a hint of despair. But the condo's interior transported Vance to a world of luxury and opulence.

Two Asian males and one female sat on cream-colored leather couches, dressed smartly, sipping expensive red wine.

Modern art adorned the walls, and the open design of the room revealed a five-star gourmet kitchen and a modern dining room.

"This is Vance Palladian," Kevin said as they approached. "Or Paladin, as his friends call him."

"You already have a warrior name?" the woman said, raising an eyebrow. She stood and held out her hand. Unsure if he should shake or kiss it, he clasped her hand with both of his, cool long fingers, manicured nails tickling his skin. "I'm Midori Nami. My friends call me Sapphire."

She smiled. Piercing blue eyes sized him up. Contacts? No doubt.

Releasing her hands, she brushed hair from her forehead. A sign of romantic interest?

Her svelte model's body betrayed a hint of athleticism, not quite fitness, not quite fashion, neatly wrapped in a long sleeve tunic with matching skirt.

He shouldn't sleep with Sho's employees. For her, he'd make an exception.

Next to her, a young man with spiky dyed blond hair gave him a firm handshake.

"*Kinryū*, the Golden Dragon," he said.

Vance turned, greeting a man he recognized, a man with a hardened face and unfashionably long hair. He held out his hand but did not rise. His leather jacket suffered from dry rot, and he sported jeans and work boots.

"*Ku-Kami*, the Ninth God," he said, his voice gravel and baritone. "You know me as Jax."

Gems, and dragons, and gods, oh my!

"What's your warrior name?" Vance asked, turning to Kevin.

"*Byakko*, the White Tiger," Kevin said. "These are Sho's greatest students."

Vance nodded.

Kevin motioned to an empty spot on the couch, and Vance took a seat.

Slipping into the dining room, Kevin returned with two glasses of wine before the silence became unbearable. Vance accepted a glass gratefully.

"We'd like you to join our group," Kevin said, sitting down. Kevin sipped his wine, allowing Vance to digest the statement.

"I'm flattered," Vance said. "I don't suppose this is a poker club."

They all laughed.

"You have a good sense of humor," Kevin said. "We've come together to help Sho."

"Help?" Vance asked, curious.

"Sho is in incredible physical shape for his age, but he's having trouble with his mind."

"Sho seemed pretty sharp to me," Vance said.

"He has long moments of clarity, but his slips are getting more frequent. He forgets things and makes poor judgments. You'll pick up on the symptoms soon enough."

"Symptoms of what?"

"Not sure. Alzheimer's, maybe. He won't see a doctor."

"How do we help him?"

"Sho made a fortune through good business deals. Been losing his fortune making bad ones. Understand what happens if Sho runs out of money?"

"I'll be unemployed."

"It's worse than that."

"Sho said his fortune keeps Jade safe."

"Precisely. Her brother has a stranglehold on the police. Sho pays off the politicians who control the police. But no money, no protection."

"Looks like Sho's still doing okay," Vance said, gesturing to the luxury apartment."

"Sho didn't pay for this," Sapphire said.

"We have business dealings of our own," the Ninth God said.

"Doesn't sound like things are on the up and up."

"They're not," Golden Dragon said.

"Not that we're doing anything bad," Kevin quickly added. "We only take from the corrupt."

"Like Robin Hood?" Vance asked.

"It's not selfless. We want to live well, have what we desire. But my greatest desire is keeping Jade safe."

"You want me to be one of your soldiers, is that it?" Vance asked.

We're inviting you into the inner circle," Sapphire said, bright blue eyes drawing him in. "The Kaiden."

"Kaiden?" Vance asked.

"The ghosts in Sho's organization," Kevin said. "Creating change, unseen. You'd be an asset to our team."

"How do you know I won't tell Sho what you're doing?"

"You might. But I doubt it. Even if you decide not to join, you can still perform your original purpose while we work in the background. We have something to show you. If you wrap your mind around this, you'll say yes. And, if we're going to go further, honesty is crucial."

The three men stood and then retreated to the dining room.

Sapphire touched Vance's shoulder. He turned, met her inviting smile with his own. Neither needed to speak.

When he heard footsteps, he looked back. Then his heart leaped into his throat. On his feet, backing up, he was ready for a fight.

Sapphire was already behind him, placing a gentle hand on his shoulder.

"Relax. No one is going to hurt you."

Four demons stood before him.

Disassociated. Confused. Adrenaline surging. He fought off fight or flight.

"Oni," Sapphire said. "They work for us."

"Were they the ones in the convenience store?" Vance asked, face flushing hot with anger.

"Yes," Sapphire said, gently turning him toward her. "Look at me."

"I don't understand," he said, searching her eyes.

When he turned back, the demons had vanished. Kevin, Golden boy, and Jax had returned.

"You attacked me?"

"Again, not us. Our associates. You weren't supposed to get involved," Kevin said. "Mistakes were made."

"This is how you make money for Sho? Rob stores in masks? Petty theft? It doesn't make sense."

"First, they're not wearing masks. Second, they were supposed to scare Jade so she wouldn't sneak off the estate again."

"Wait?" Vance said. "What do you mean they weren't wearing masks?"

"Make a choice, Vance," Kevin said. "Come with us. Be one of us and have all your questions answered. Or stay in ignorance. The choice is yours."

Vance followed the Kaiden to the roof. Even in darkness, Vance could make out the sloped avian coup.

Kevin reached inside and withdrew a crow. Vance blinked. In the half-light, it looked like the crow had three legs. Impossible.

"The crow will sacrifice for you. She will shed her blood for you."

"You're crazy," Vance said. These people belonged in an asylum.

"One drop of blood to trigger the transformation. Come on, Vance. Are you chicken?"

All the men laughed.

"You don't have to do this," Sapphire said. "Once done, there's no going back."

"Yeah, right? Whatever," Vance said, pulling away from her. "Let's complete the initiation so I can see what's really going on."

Kevin smiled. He retrieved a pocketknife, lifted the bird while Vance squatted, positioning himself underneath.

A slight cut and a single blood droplet found his tongue. Cherry blossoms. Kevin released the bird. The crow flittered into the darkness.

Vance felt different. Power surged through him. Around him, the Kaiden disrobed. Like in a dream, Vance followed their lead. Naked from the waist up, they grew wings. He felt them spout from his back, transforming into an anthropomorphic bird-like creature. A human hybrid of some sort. Indistinct in the darkness, he couldn't see their faces. The Kaiden ascended, and he followed, buzzing the trees that bordered the property and flying into the night.

Vance couldn't believe he was flying. Couldn't believe what the Kaiden had become. He was one of them. The wind whipped around him, a turbulence not easily navigable. He needed to concentrate to stay stable in the air.

"What are we?" Vance said when he finally felt comfortable flying straight ahead.

"Tengu," Kevin said. "Crow demons. We brought war to the world. We birthed the ninja."

They flew through the darkness until they reached Providence. Below them the square roof of a building looked smaller than expected.

"The first thing you need to do is learn to land on a building," Kevin said. "It will take some getting used to."

Vance descended too quickly.

Shit!

He hit the building hard, peddling his feet, finding no traction, he landed on his back. Vance sucked wind.

"Not good," The Ninth God said.

"We need to teach you how to receive the ground," Kevin said.

They were in the air again. Vance's confidence had fled.

"The first time is always the most difficult," Sapphire said. "Slow your descent. Think about landing safely and you will."

Easier said than done, Vance thought.

This time as he dropped, he splayed out his wings, feeling the wind like a shelf holding him aloft, slowing his descent. He squinted and gritted his teeth. Landed on the roof in stride until coming to a stop.

"Not bad," The Ninth God said, reluctantly.

"Better than most on their second try," Kevin said. "A few more flights and you should be good to go."

The Kaiden flew into the dark sky, and Vance followed.

Chapter Seven

The alarm jarred Vance from a deep sleep. In the dream, he had become a crow demon, a tengu. Last night had only been a dream. He looked at the clock bleary eyed until the red numbers came into focus. 4:30 a.m. It was going to be a long day.

By force of will, he swung his feet to the floor. His muscles didn't feel sore as much as tight. His body reacted to exercise this way after a layover. Tomorrow, the pain would kick in. In a week or two, the soreness would recede as his body adapted.

In the shower, he counted his bruises, allowing the hot water to work into his muscles. The invigorating hydrotherapy revitalized his mind, awakened his senses. He slowly twisted the faucet until the water turned lukewarm, then jacked it up again.

The shower reduced the negative effects of over exercising. A slight rotation of the spigot and the spray turned cold, shocking his system, closing his pores, and putting out the small fire Sapphire had lit the night before. He shut off the water, shivered, and then toweled off.

After a light breakfast, he and Kevin ascended the trail using the technique of *mu no ho*, silent running. Vance felt stronger than yesterday, and more purposeful. Last night was a shadow.

He worked his basic blocks and strikes again on the hill and then followed Kevin to the tree line.

"This is your tree," Kevin said. The tree was wrapped with straw and overlaid with cloth to make a safe, striking surface. "Time for *atemi no tanren*, strike conditioning."

"What did the tree do to me?" Vance asked.

Kevin laughed.

"In olden times, warriors practiced outside, using nature to condition their bodies. As you get stronger, and hit harder, you'll wonder what you did to the tree."

After a period of intensive training, Kevin stopped him. Vance bent over to slow his heart rate, sweat dripping as he controlled his breathing.

"You've performed the basics. Combined with your past training, you'll be formidable. You'll need lots of repetition to reprogram your muscle memory."

Vance nodded as his respiration returned to normal, blinking salty sweat from red eyes. Good training came down to repetition. In a real encounter, there wasn't time to think. Muscle memory was everything. And Kevin was right, Vance felt a lot more powerful.

It wouldn't be long before he'd be back with Jax and the prison crew. Vance hoped he could avoid a confrontation.

After breakfast, Vance made his way back to the sprawling estate. He knew plenty of work awaited him and the crew.

"I was going to have you mulch," Jax said. "But Slade seems riled today."

"I can hold my own," Vance said, but it was just his ego talking. No reason for a confrontation with a guy who had nothing to lose.

"Okay, mulch for a while," Jax said. "But I'm keeping my eye out. You're not ready to deal with him. Not yet."

That's what you get for opening your damn mouth.

Vance remembered what drove him to the martial arts. He had come home to an empty house. He was a teen, many years before his dad and his stepmother had met their untimely deaths. So much tragedy in his life. Why did it seem to follow him?

He didn't tell his friends his folks were on a short vacation. He had done that once, decided to invite a small group to a party and half the school had shown up. His parents finally trusted him again. He didn't want to screw that up.

He had dropped his friends off after a night of drinking. There hadn't been anything to do in his old hometown, and he had acted as the designated driver.

In those days they cruised around, pouring rum into McDonalds coke and hung around until the rent-a-cop made them leave.

When he returned home, he found the front door ajar. *Had someone broken in? Had he forgotten to lock the damn thing and the wind popped it open?*

Slowly, he pushed the door open and peered into the darkness of his home. His hackles rose. An overwhelming fear, a panic, gripped him. Wouldn't let go.

He backed away and tried to slow his heart. He wouldn't realize until later that he had had a panic attack.

The police arrived and inventoried the burglary. It had been a quick snatch and grab. They got some money and his stepmother's jewelry. He still lived with the guilt. The break-in never would have happened if he had been home. Yet, more powerful than the guilt was that terrible overpowering fear. He never wanted to feel that way again.

Within weeks of the incident, he had joined Gold's Tae Kwon Do and began forging his body so that fear would never enter him again.

He knew now that fear provided a healthy warning, a signal to pay attention, stay alert, and either fight or flee.

The hard training had helped him master his fear.

Why was he afraid now?

Why were all these old ghosts returning to haunt him? He didn't like it.

Vance lifted the backend of a wheelbarrow filled with mulch and a shovel, wheeled it to the same area by the mansion he had worked on yesterday.

He looked up, hoping to see Jade staring down from the window. Immediately, he felt embarrassed for the longing.

"What ya looking at?" Slade said behind him. Vance recognized his voice. "Looking for someone?"

Vance's face flushed. His fists clenched around the shovel. He spun around to face Slade.

Jax, the Ninth God, was suddenly there as well, like he had materialized out of thin air.

"Move along, Slade," Jax said. Slade nodded his head. Vance felt the overwhelming urge to knock Slade's sly grin off his face.

"You come with me," Jax said to Vance.

Vance tossed his shovel and followed.

His anger subsided as he left the hot sun behind and entered Jax's dojo. A shroud covered what looked like a statue underneath. The human shape made Vance's skin crawl.

"I can't be everywhere and see everything," Jax said handing him a sharp instrument wrapped in duct tape, an improvised prison shank. "So, I need to prepare you for all eventualities."

Vance took the weapon. Jax's warmth still clung to the hard plastic.

"You want to be on the lookout for shit like this," Jax said, referring to the shank.

"Why don't I just change," Vance said, then felt funny saying it. "You know. Like we do at night."

"That's the problem. We can only do that at night."

Jax approached the form in the middle of the room and whipped off the covering. A ballistics gel shaped human figure propped up by a metal stand that allowed it to remain upright, waited for him. The thing looked like something from Vlad the Impaler's dungeon.

Jax pointed out all the main arteries on the lifelike mannequin.

"You'll want to protect these areas if he attacks you. These are also the locations where, if you cut or stab him, he will bleed out the fastest, ending the fight."

Vance hoped it wouldn't come to that, but a secret side of him, a dark side wanted it to happen, wanted to take Slade's life, show him who was boss, who really ruled the roost.

Those thoughts bordered on insanity. Or, at least, sociopathy. Real violence wasn't a cathartic fantasy. It wasn't romantic. The aftermath was permanent.

Vance began his practice by moving around the mannequin making the stabs, like Jax showed him, to the vital points without penetrating the gel. After hundreds of flicking repetitions, Jax stopped him.

"Now do it for real," Jax said.

Vance attacked the stationary human target slamming the makeshift blade in repeatedly, fake blood spurting over faux flesh and onto his hand.

A low growl emitted from deep in his chest as he slashed again and again. His slashes turned into stabs, and he continued until, if the target had been a living human, that person would be very dead, indeed.

"Very good," Jax said, ending the session. "You will be ready."

"I feel different," Vance said in between heavy gasps.

"You have let out your inner demon," Jax said.

But Vance felt more like he had let one in.

Back at the cottage, Vance pan-fried a hamburger and baked a handful of frozen French fries. Steamed frozen microwave broccoli made it all healthy, he mused. The food renewed and refreshed him.

After dinner, a black dogi awaited him on the bed, his black belt had been tied around the uniform, folded neatly and traditionally.

He untied the belt and donned the crisp new canvas uniform. Putting on the dogi felt good, luxurious, as if it had been tailored just for him. He slipped on a pair of black tabi boots, that had been placed by the bed, and draped the black belt over his shoulders.

Vance trekked up the hill toward the Teahouse Dojo. The light had just started to fade, but he knew his day had only just begun.

Inside, the unmistakable smell of sweat and feet intermingled in the air of the small space. Not surprisingly, having spent so many years in martial arts schools, he found the scent comforting. Sho awaited him silently and alone in the windowless dojo.

Vance turned his back to Sho and tied his belt around his waist, a sign of respect in Korean martial arts training. He turned back around and walked toward Sho.

Sho matched Vance's stride, smiling widely. As Sho closed the distance, he extended his hand in warm greeting. Vance found himself mirroring Sho's expression and movement, extending his own hand. Vance felt Sho's talon grip and knew he had made a mistake. He had misjudged the situation.

Sho turned Vance's hand up and in a counterclockwise motion painfully locking Vance's whole arm, and then, with quickness and grace, stepped under Vance's armpit and through to the other side. Vance felt his feet leave the floor. The room flip-flopped. Vance landed on his back, sucking wind, unable to breath, as if the tatami mats had reached up and attacked him.

When will I learn?

"I really need to teach you ukemi, how to receive the ground," Sho said as he stared down at his student. Everyone was saying that to him lately. The look on Sho's face was one of pity.

"Why did you do that?" Vance asked once he could breathe again, trying to shake off the rage that percolated in his veins, an anger stronger than his morning coffee. He sat up and then forced himself to stand, feeling, at that moment, much older than his thirty-five years.

"That was your first lesson, Mr. Palladian," Sho said with a devious tinge to his voice. "I just exploited an automatic societal response, used it against you."

"I've learned techniques like that as defenses against someone crushing your hand."

"Yes. When you study a classical martial art, you think of yourself as the good guy defending yourself or others. When you practice our tradition, you must think of yourself as the bad guy."

"Why would you do that?" Vance asked, truly perplexed. He had thought of himself as a protector for so long that he couldn't imagine why he would want to wear a different mask.

"You can't hope to defend against someone with bad intentions unless you experience them yourself. But you must be careful. When you walk on the shadowy side, your vision is easily obscured."

"So, this is all part of your ryu's training?"

"Yes. This is how our ancestors could metaphorically see through the darkness, the shadows that obscure the average person's vision, and by turning it around on his adversary, cloud men's minds." Sho said. "I would love to teach you the whole of our tradition, but to do that I would have to break you of your Tae Kwon Do Karate style habits and teach you a new and subtle way of moving."

"How long would it take to do that?" Vance asked, eager to throw himself into a new art and a new challenge. After all, if he was going to do something, he wanted to do it all the way.

"Ten years to make you proficient in the principles and another five before you could actually use the fighting system in real life."

Vance wondered at the hyperbole of the statement, but Sho's facial expression betrayed nothing but frankness.

"Then how will you teach me?"

"The same way I instructed Kevin to begin your training. I will build upon your foundation and teach you how to use what you already know in life and death combat. Speaking of what you know, I want to see how much of Kevin's lessons you've absorbed. I want to see how you deal with an attacker punching you."

"I'll be happy to show you," Vance said feeling confident.

"Behind you, Mr. Palladian!"

Vance turned in time to see a blur of an oni bearing down on him. *Where did he come from?*

Vance had no idea. The attacker's fist shot out, and it was all Vance could do just to get his hands up in time. Knuckles contacted his jaw sending his brain swimming, knocking him to the floor. Vance's jaw throbbed and his mouth tasted like he had spent all day sucking on a 9-volt battery.

"Lesson number two of real combat: move out of the way of the punch before you attempt to block, parry, or strike," Sho said, his voice sounded as if emitted from an echo chamber. The room spun for a moment and then righted itself.

"Lesson number three: keep your teeth clenched as if you were wearing a mouth guard. Unless, of course, you like having your jaw dislocated and all your teeth knocked out. Though, I understand it can be quite entertaining drinking all your meals through a straw."

Real funny, Vance thought. Sho was turning out to be quite the comedian. *Why did I decide to do this?*

Vance's teeth ached and his cheek swelled. His muscles week, he forced himself to stand.

The young Japanese man wore an oni mask and could only be described as slight of build, and yet his punch packed a major wallop. Was it a mask? He couldn't be sure.

"You must always expect the unexpected," Sho said. "Awareness is everything. You'll get it in time.

"Use your cat stance and instead of moving forward or back like they teach you in TKD, I want you to retreat diagonally."

The oni threw another punch. Vance turned his body while thrusting his arms toward the corner of the room allowing the momentum of his movement to pull him out of his attacker's range. He landed with ninety percent of his weight on his back leg and ten on his front, resembling the posture of a cat. Then as the punch sailed inches from his head, Vance struck the underside of his opponent's arm, batting up to render it temporarily useless.

The oni attacked with his other hand, rocketing out another punch. Vance moved out of the way, repeating the striking technique, hearing the demon expel air.

"Good!" Sho said. "Now, instead of jerking yourself out of the way, subtlety shift your feet and slip past the punch or kick."

The oni repeated the one-two attack.

A big smile brightened Vance's face. He couldn't help it. Just by subtly shifting his feet and body he couldn't be hit no matter how fast his attacker punched.

"Sometimes graceful slowness can trump speed, but don't get too cocky, Mr. Palladian," Sho said. "You'll find it much more difficult to do when an opponent is committed to taking your head off."

The next night, after dinner, Vance trudged up the hill again and entered the Teahouse Dojo.

"Tonight," Sho said. "We shall work on Combat Judo. I will show you five techniques."

"Sounds intense," Vance said, feeling curious.

"Judo was formulated by Jigero Kano. Kano Sensei had distilled the techniques from Japanese battlefield jujutsu systems. He wanted to create an art that could be practiced safely, or at least more safely. Chuck Norris found his way to Korean Karate because he broke his back during Judo training.

True. Vance knew that story well.

"What I will show you here, you could never use in a sporting competition."

Then Sho gave the floor to the oni who began the training by showing Vance how to receive the ground using Ukemi, rolling and break-falling techniques.

Vance performed front rolls, back rolls, side rolls, and break falls.

"These basics will keep you relatively safe in the dojo," Sho said. "Eventually we'll teach you how to roll over hard surfaces, up hills, and over obstacles. You can also roll to attack an opponent or drop to the ground at night to escape and disappear from sight."

Then, to begin the grappling portion of the class, Sho grabbed Vance by his shoulders, turning his arms like turning a steering wheel he forced Vance's upper body to his right. Vance felt his left leg come free from the floor. As he met the force and tried to regain his balance, he felt the inside of Sho's foot strike the side of his shin. He completely lost his balance and hit the ground.

"That was *DeAshi Harai*, a basic foot sweep," Sho said looking down at him. "Notice that, instead of a sweep, I could have stomped down diagonally on the outside of your shin if I wanted to break it."

Vance rolled back and up to a standing position and grabbed Sho in a ten and four position, hand grasping onto the uniform under the triceps, the other hand just above the elbow.

Sho did the same except he seized Vance's flesh through the canvass of the uniform. The sudden shock of pain forced Vance to cry out.

Distracted, Vance didn't see Sho release his right hand and stab his thumb underneath Vance's collar bone, pushing him off balance, breaking his structure.

Vance grimaced as his nerves registered the pain. Then Sho moved to the outside of Vance's lead leg and swept him. Vance felt the vacuum of weightlessness as he was up righted and then gravity kicked in and he met the floor, slapping out to dissipate the falls concussion. Even with the precautionary technique, Vance's body still throbbed from the impact.

"How did that feel?" Sho asked.

Not very good.

"Getting up is the hardest part," Vance said.

"That is a variation of *Osoto gari*, the large outer reap. In real life you would augment the technique to crush his pelvis. Of course, don't do that to your training partner. If you break him, who would you train with?"

"Of course," Vance said, and then laughed nervously.

Then Sho showed him *Ogoshi* a hip throw and Vance greeted the floor again.

Vance was instructed to toss the oni so that he could roll out safely but was also shown how to throw an attacker on his back to take his wind, or onto his head to break his neck.

The last technique was called *Seoi Nage*, over the shoulder throw.

"What's the fifth technique?

"The fifth technique is *Ku* the void realm," Sho said. "It's the ability to use any combination of these techniques freely in sparring or in actual combat. It's not something I can show you. It's a state of mind. You must find it yourself."

Vance took to the techniques readily, sure that something so practical would come in handy. Then the oni stopped being compliant. Vance bounced off the tatami mats enough times to consider buying stock in ibuprofen. Finally, he solved the riddle and began besting the demon.

Escapes from throws were taught next, so they couldn't be used against him. The techniques had him cartwheeling and contorting to escape or reverse the throw.

Vance felt spent at the end of the training and happy to be done.

"Tomorrow, I want you to run up the hill alone," Sho said. "A test awaits."

After eating in silence, with only his tired mind for company, Vance prepared to retire. He took a quick shower and then brushed his teeth. Entering the bedroom, he found a pair of camouflage pants, a matching shirt, and a pair of tabi neatly laid on the bed.

What are these for?

Too tired to care, he tossed everything on the floor and went to bed. He awoke moments before the alarm sounded.

Outside, he took a deep breath of the cool morning air and wondered what Sho had in store for him. *Hide and go seek, maybe?* With Sho, anything was possible.

As he reached the trail, he broke into a run. At the top of the path, he found Sho waiting for him instead of Kevin. Sho wore the same style woodland camo. Vance realized this was the first time he had ever seen Sho in anything except a business suit. But Vance was more intrigued by what Sho held in his hand.

"Archery?" Vance asked, as he approached.

"Hunting," Sho said handing him the bow. A quiver filled with arrows was slung over his shoulder. "It is a necessary part of the training. Warriors have hunted since time immemorial."

"What type of animals are we hunting?" Vance asked. The whole idea seemed foreign and archaic. He had always gotten food from the supermarket.

"Come with me," Sho said. He led Vance past the straw wrapped tree and into the woods.

Sho moved unhindered through the forest, making little noise. Vance tried to do the same, but his gait mimicked a herd of elephants.

Vance saw an animal grazing up ahead in an open clearing, a white-tailed deer. As they moved closer the animal paid them no mind. He couldn't understand how they were sneaking up on this creature. Even if the beast couldn't hear Sho, Vance didn't think he would have escaped notice.

Then, as they approached the clearing, Vance realized the deer was nothing more than a decoy, or by the holes in the body—a target.

Sho tutored him on how to thread the arrow, pull it back, and aim. Vance practiced while Sho gave him more instruction.

Then Vance climbed the rough branches and pulled himself onto a tree stand that had been erected for just such a purpose.

Sho stood on tiptoe and passed the bow and quiver to him. Sho moved out of the way, disappearing behind Vance's tree.

"Take your time, Mr. Palladian," Sho called to him. "Let the bow become part of you. Then release. The hunter and the hunted must become one."

Vance breathed, and reaching the peak of his inhalation, he exhaled and let the arrow fly. He watched in dismay as the arrow stuck into the earth a few feet behind the animal.

Damn!

"Try again," Sho said.

Vance breathed deeply and shifted on the platform.

This was the last thing he wanted to be doing. He pushed away at the thoughts that invaded, thoughts of the Kaiden, thoughts of the tengu.

Again, Vance went through each step and then let the arrow fly. This time the arrow hit the ground two feet in front of the target.

"That's much better," Sho said. "Breath like the earth. Become one with your surroundings."

Vance thought about the instructions as he removed another arrow from the quiver. *Breath like the earth?* He tamped down his frustration and remembered the first day with Kevin on the bluff. He needed to feel that way again.

Vance cleared his mind and inhaled deeply, the air then rushing out as if it were escaping a cavern. The whole world vibrated around him as he felt the connection. Tunnel vision. Now he could only see the target. He released the arrow.

Seemingly moving in slow motion, the feathers bristling in the wind, the arrow found its mark, a three-inch area that represented the animal's heart—a humane kill.

"Very good, Mr. Palladian!" Sho said. "Well done!"

Vance released another arrow. It hit inches from the first.

Perfect!

Then another.

Beginners luck?

He didn't want to doubt himself.

"Hold fire," Sho said, returning to the decoy and dragging it away. "I'll be right back."

Vance waited in the tree, wondering what would happen next. He figured he'd have to stay perched up there all day, maybe even part of the night, before a deer crossed his path.

Minutes later, Sho returned. He led a doe by a leash to the same location as where the decoy had been previously. Sho pounded a spike into the soft earth and secured the leash to it. Pulling apple slices from his pockets, he placed the fruit on the ground and the doe got busy eating.

"That's not very sporting," Vance said, feeling a queasiness in the pit of his stomach.

"We don't have time to be sporting," Sho said. "If you'd like to camp here for a few nights, I've stocked the grounds with white tales...."

"I guess I better just get it over with," Vance said. It was like hunting at a petting zoo.

"Good decision," Sho said. "If it makes you feel any better, I will donate the meat from the animal to a local food bank."

Even though he thought it should, Sho's act of generosity didn't quell his reluctance. Vance didn't harbor any animosity against hunters, he had just never done the deed and could have gone his whole life without needing to take an animal's life.

Sho moved away signaling the beginning of the exercise.

Feeling his heart accelerating, Vance removed an arrow from his quiver. He threaded the arrow and pulled it taut until the feathers were parallel with his ear. He sighted the kill spot, took a deep breath, and then let it out. If his aim wasn't true, the animal would suffer needlessly.

He released and watched as the arrow hit its target. The doe bucked in pain, attempted to run off but the tether jerked her back and dumped her to the ground.

"Quickly Mr. Palladian," Sho said.

Vance didn't hesitate, he leapt from the tree, bending his knees to absorb the impact.

Sho tossed a large hunting knife to him.

"Put her out of her misery."

Catching the knife by its handle, Vance pursed his lips to seal his resolve. He sprung upon the dying animal, found a spot just below her collar and slit her throat. Hot blood spilled from the wound, and he watched the light go out in the frightened animal's eyes.

"Very good, Mr. Palladian," Sho said, "The lesson is over for today."

Vance nodded and stood up. He had had enough stress for one day. Killing the animal had appeased the demon growing inside. He felt the rise of a bolder confidence. This would not be a good day for Slade to mess with him. Not a good day at all.

"I've heard rumors," Jax said, handing Vance a tactical folding knife.

"What do I need this for?" Vance asked, but he already knew. Slade would be looking for him. He flicked the blade out by pushing up on the thumb stud. The blade was coated with a black corrosion resistant coating to keep the steel from rusting. The point ground into a chiseled *tanto*, a superior style for combat, with the rear of the blade serrated to make the cuts more efficient.

"If something happens," Jax said. "Think of the knife as an anti-grappling measure."

Vance didn't know what Jax meant, but he had an idea. He didn't like it. Even so, he slipped the knife into the back of his jeans, threading the clip onto the material so it wouldn't fall out.

There wasn't anything else to say. Time to get back to work. Grabbing a tricked out gas-powered lawnmower, Vance pushed it over to an embankment where the top was a little too steep for a riding mower.

Two ropes had been attached to the handle. He carefully unwound them, laying the ends on the grass.

Pulling the starter cord, the mower roared to life. He'd have to think about getting a pair of earplugs. He didn't want to go deaf.

Vance lowered the mower down the embankment until it reached the line where the riding mower couldn't continue. Down was easy. Up, not so much. He heaved the rope, the machine reluctantly responding. Then let the rope slacken, sending it back down.

He had just gotten the hang of the process when a hard blow to his jaw sent him to the ground. He tasted metal, as blood dribbled down his chin.

Vance's head swam.

Slade jumped on him, taking his wind, raining down blows like some prison version of MMA ground-and-pound.

Panic hit him now.

He lifted his body up to control the space, finding a reprieve from Slade's smack down. His abs burned. He wouldn't be able to do this for long. He had to launch a counter measure.

Vance retrieved the knife and thumbed it open. Now he knew what Jax wanted him to do. He could stab Slade easily. Kill him. That would stop him.

Vance couldn't do it. He wasn't ready to take a life.

Slade hit him. No pain, just concussion.

Another hit. He felt pain with that one.

Then Jax was above him, tossing Slade to the grass.

Slade scrambled away.

Powerful hands pulled Vance to his feet.

The other prisoners watched with stony expressions. One walked down the embankment, shutting off the mower.

"Sho was wrong," Jax said. "You're not the one."

The prisoners' expressions didn't change, they returned to what they had been doing before, as if nothing had happened.

"Lesson's over," Jax said. "Go back and clean up."

Vance nodded. Defeated. He needed more than a shower. He needed a strong drink.

Chapter Eight

Keikan ran the security guard's picture through a local criminal database. Came up empty.

With a name, he could have searched the Rhode Island Judiciary website's Criminal Information Search Database. All court information was in the public domain, allowing anyone to search basic court records.

Without a name, Keikan had no choice but to farm out the check to the FBI. Hopefully, they'd find something and get back to him quickly. He had to laugh at that. Could a federal government bureaucracy do anything quickly? He'd love to be around when it happened.

He filled the morning with paperwork, doing his best to tune out the conversations which bled through the useless cubical walls. Around 1 p.m., he brought Hayden to lunch, hoping a full belly would fend off the old crank's nihilistic attitude. It didn't.

After lunch, Hayden drove back toward the Public Safety Complex.

Keikan's smartphone vibrated. He fished it out. Looked at the reminder notification. He would have forgotten.

"You coming tonight?" Keikan asked. He already knew the answer.

"I'm too old for that shit," Hayden said. "You have fun. I'm getting home at a reasonable hour… for once."

A large situation room was in the basement directly under the dungeon. Before Keikan had procured it, the space was rarely used. The main area, originally cluttered with folding tables, chairs, and a podium, now stood empty. Only the polished wooden floor remained. Floodlights on the ceiling provided plenty of light.

After donning a traditional white dogi uniform in the adjoining locker and shower room, Keikan approached the far wall where hung an 8 1/2 by 24 inch sheet of parchment framed and sealed under glass. He read it before every training session as a reminder.

When Keikan had decided he wanted to teach defensive tactics and self-defense, he knew he needed to instill the proper ethics into the officers. He didn't want to give them techniques that could injure and not provide them a code of conduct within which to operate. He had seen how the martial arts in the hands of the wrong people could change their personality and make them a threat to, instead of a protector of, society. Thus, he created what became known as Keikan's Decalogue.

Keikan's Decalogue

Take responsibility for your actions. Exercise control in training and in life.
Train regularly, allowing enough time for rest and recovery.
Persevere and complete what you start.
Be flexible in both body and mind.
Defeat your enemy but leave him his life.
Forge your character through hard training and always aim to act honorably.
Your teacher and training partners are your martial arts family. Be loyal and treat them fairly.
Do not compare your progress with others. Be the best that you can be.
Live your life as a protector. Defend the weak and the helpless.
Cultivate an unconquerable fighting spirit.
Obey the laws you have sworn to uphold.

The students trickled in, dayshift sergeants, off duty beat-cops, and a few who were riding their desks.

Most nights he taught *goshen jujutsu*, self-defense, within the rules of engagement that law enforcement was forced to operate. Cops could grab and restrain, but punching and kicking could get an officer into major legal trouble.

Tonight, however, he would train their spirits.

Following Keikan's example, each officer stopped and read the Decalogue before entering the locker room to change.

Once ready, the class lined up single file, all wearing full Kendo armor and carrying bamboo swords.

One by one, they attacked him. His speed startling, his blows disrupting their momentum. All they could do was shake their heads, hide the stinging pain of the bamboo, and get back in line for another thrashing.

When he had finished throttling his fellow officers, his satisfied grin remained hidden behind the kendo facemask.

They paired up and worked techniques for the rest of the session. The clack of bamboo kendo swords clashing echoed through the training hall.

"That's it for tonight," he said as he removed his mask. "See you all next week."

The class dispersed to the locker rooms. He saw no reason for traditional formalities. Everyone had been through police academy training. They didn't need another dose of it.

Keikan motioned to one officer, Paul Finnegan, a tall and wiry transplant from Boston. Although twenty-five, he still retained a baby face and freckles.

"Yeah, boss?" Finnegan asked, traversing the distance.

"You'd always have my back, right?" Keikan asked. "If anything ever went down?"

"Yeah, sure," Finnegan said. "Why wouldn't I?"

"Off the books?"

"You know me," Finnegan said with a wide grin. "Always looking for a little action."

"I need people I can trust," Keikan said. "I have two in mind. Need a couple more. Only officers who've trained with us, live by the code, but will work outside the system."

"Can do," Finnegan said.

"Good," Keikan said. "Next class we'll all hang back and I'll give a sitrep."

Finnegan nodded then turned and walked to the locker room. Keikan kept a poker face as the officers streamed out of the locker room nodding to him. He nodded in return. His plan was working perfectly. This was a game, a game of strategy, and a contest that he would win.

Chapter Nine

Sho's eyes looked vacant. His expression slackened. His train of thought derailed. He stared beyond the Teahouse Dojo, a realm only he could see.

"*Sensei*?" Vance asked.

Sho shook out the cobwebs. His eyes shone bright again. He had returned.

"I'm sorry," Sho said, face reddening. "Where were we?"

"You were about to show sword techniques," Vance said. It was the first time he had seen Sho like this. Maybe Kevin was right.

"Yes. Yes, that is right," Sho said, a tight smile pulling at his lips. "*Hiden Jutsu*. The hidden sword.

"Use the same movement as an outside block to draw your weapon. We call this *biken*, the secret sword. Perform your blocks and strikes as if drawing a sword. Funakoshi, the founder of Shotokan Karate, said this once."

Sho had Vance tie on an *obi* sword belt, and then taught him to draw the sword, careful to pull the saya scabbard gently away from the live blade so as not to cut through the thin material.

With the same motion, Vance was to make his first cut as soon as the live blade had been released.

After Vance had some time to practice, Sho taught him various sword cuts using his Tae Kwon Do blocks as a base. Vance couldn't help but continue to be amazed at what was hidden in the basics, secrets obscured in plain sight.

"You're picking this up quickly," Sho said, after watching Vance for a short time. "Still, if you face a trained swordsman, you will lose."

"That doesn't sound encouraging."

"It's not," Sho said. "A couple of tricks will help. A Japanese sword fighter always advances on the right side. The left hand guides the cut."

Sho demonstrated the standard cutting motion, gently pulling back on the bottom of the *tsuka* handle to leverage the cut.

"Reversing your grip," Sho said, switching hands, "Creates the illusion you're an amateur, deceiving the experienced warrior. This allows for alternative cuts that the swordsmen will not anticipate."

"Interesting," Vance said. "What's the other trick?"

"Look closely at my weapon, Mr. Palladian. "What do you see?"

Vance examined the sword. He couldn't see anything unusual.

What was Sho hiding?

Then it came to him.

More secrets hidden in plain sight.

"The handle is full-sized, but the blade is shorter than normal."

"Yes!" Sho said. "Good eye. The scabbard itself is full-sized as well."

"Why a full-sized scabbard for a short sword?" Vance asked.

"Yes, why indeed," Sho said. "What is the tactical advantage of a shorter sword and a longer scabbard?"

"A quicker draw?" Vance asked.

"Precisely! Your opponent's timing will be off. You'll get the jump on him."

"How are these tricks applicable in modern times?" Vance asked.

"Principles are timeless, Mr. Palladian," Sho said. "Understand them and they will serve you well."

Vance nodded, but he didn't truly understand.

"Before we call it a night, try to cut me down."

"These are live swords," Vance said, his stomach knotting.

"Danger is important for the exercise. Fully commit, and trust that I'll get out of the way."

Vance didn't like it. Risking death in training seemed foolish and unnecessary.

Sho stood in front of him. "Whenever you're ready."

Vance raised the sword into the *jodan* position, lifting the blade above his head.

Vance charged, making the cut, a cut that would split his teacher in two.

At the last second, Sho shifted his feet, evading the cut. Vance recovered, reacquired the target, and launched a second attack. The thought that this contest had become a game of life and death receded.

Sho repositioned and parried Vance's sword with the blunt side so as not to bevel the cutting edge. Vance barely noticed the harsh clash of steel on steel.

Vance spun counterclockwise, freeing his blade. Launched a third attack. Sho parried a touch too slowly, perhaps age catching up with him, focus dissipating from oncoming mental disease. Vance now had full leverage to make an attack.

Vance stopped short. Not from control, but fear.

A concealed dagger hidden in the handle of Sho's sword, now pointed at Vance's eyes.

"War is deception," Sho said. "Nothing is what it seems."

Chapter Ten

As if in a dream, Vance flew again. The others floated in formation around him, creating a barrier, keeping him from wandering off, getting lost. The night air was refreshingly cool.

Vance followed as they landed, perching on the darkened roof. How easy it was to touchdown on the ledge. Any fear of heights he had when fully human had evaporated.

Across the street stood a neon-lit building, garish light surrounded by darkness. The Dancing Hour, a gentleman's club stood as a monument to sin.

"We provide protection to our clientele," Kevin said in tengu form. "When they fall behind on payments, we remind them of our arrangement."

"Provide protection?" Vance asked. "You mean shake down the joint?"

The Golden Dragon smiled. The Ninth God stared stoically into the darkness. Sapphire squirmed.

"Look, Vance, these are bad people. They exploit their workers and make money providing to the baser needs of their patrons. Don't feel bad for them. We'd never hurt an innocent. Besides, we're doing this for Jade. To keep her safe."

Vance didn't like it. The whole thing seemed beyond sleazy. At first, he wondered if they were going to watch the dancers. Instead, they were going inside to do what? Rough somebody up? Yet, a darker side, an animalistic instinct he didn't want to acknowledge, became exhilarated by thoughts of sex and violence.

Vance took a deep breath to calm his excitement.

"Hang back," Kevin said, turning to them. "I'll talk to Tommy."

Kevin descended into the shadows. He returned to human form and approached Tommy, a big man wearing a leather jacket. They conversed just out of earshot. The bouncer gestured as he spoke, his hands becoming frenzied as the conversation continued, frustration coloring his face.

Tommy's hands shot out as if to push Kevin, knock him back, show him who was boss.

Kevin slipped to the right, grabbed Tommy's hand, and twisted it, locking the wrist as he turned his body counterclockwise. *Kote Gaeshi*, outer wrist turning throw.

Tommy's feet left the ground, somersaulted, and landed on his back. He lay on the pavement floundering like a fish plucked out of the ocean, trying to suck oxygen from a dry world.

Kevin waved them on.

They descended, gliding on membranous wings.

The amalgam of Vance's physical features combined with the tengu's exaggerated deep brow ridges, sunken eyes, and ridged horns merged human with demon to create a terrifying visage.

What had he become? The Kaiden had been his enemy. Their soldiers had put him in the hospital. Now he not only embraced their philosophy but their methodology.

Kevin transformed; his image marked by bold dark stripes of the white tiger. Triangular horns stood in for ears.

Black and gold skin and high eyebrow arches gave the Golden Dragon the visage of a mythical beast.

The Ninth God's face shone a terrible alabaster, as if a grimacing skeleton had combined with a grinning bird demon, horns sprouting from either side of his head.

Sapphire looked back at him, her face still strangely beautiful, an amalgam of delicate femininity juxtaposed by fierceness. Her piercing blue eyes reflected seduction. Tenderness when looking at him, cruelty when she turned away.

A thumping bass grew louder as they approached the establishment.

Entering the building, the music deafened. Gel lights painted the club, obscuring the patrons in red and orange.

On the stage, a red-haired woman danced topless, undulating perfectly with the beat, a siren using her body as song.

Vance forced himself to return his gaze to Kevin, who strode toward the back room.

Another bouncer, a big bald guy in a dark t-shirt made a beeline for Kevin, cutting him off.

Without stopping, Kevin kicked the bald bouncer through a door. Vance couldn't hear the splintering of wood over the music.

Stepping across the unconscious bouncer, the Kaiden stormed into a dimly lit hallway and past a surgically enhanced bottle blonde. She flattened herself against the wall to allow them passage, eyes wide with terror, before hightailing it out of there.

Kevin kicked open the last door on the right. This time Vance heard the impact.

"Rico," Kevin said as they filed into the room.

Rico's office stood sparsely furnished. The walls sported 1970s wood paneling and would have remained frozen in time if not for the framed poster boards. Advertisements of famous dancers and porn stars who had performed at The Hour in recent years. Two dented metal file cabinets adorned the far wall.

Rico stood behind a battered wooden desk.

He had unceremoniously pushed a pile of folders onto the floor to make room for four lines of white powder. Rico's straw hand shook.

"Kevin, my friend," Rico said, his voice steadier than Vance would have imagined under the circumstances. "Just about to have a pick-me-up. I have plenty for all."

"You can spend your money on that shit? You can pay up."

"It was a…a gift from the girls. Business has been down. You know the economy."

"I've been patient. The Italians would have already broken your fingers. No telling what the Chinese would do."

"Yeah, you're probably right," Rico said, his forehead shiny with sweat. "You have been good to us."

Rico made a quick move, deliberate and smooth, producing a snub-nosed .38 from his desk. Kevin moved quicker. Sharp *shurikan* star blades pinwheeled through the air. They bit into the flesh of Rico's chest and arms.

Rico screamed and dropped the gun. The grinding thump of bass ensured the customers would never hear him. Blood soaked through Rico's button-down oxford shirt.

"You sound like I'm killing you," Kevin said as he strode toward him. He scooped up the pistol and hid it in his waistband. Then he grabbed Rico by the throat. "You're worth more to me alive than dead, but don't push your luck."

Rico hastily rattled off a set of numbers. Kevin walked directly to a framed poster, removed it from the wall, revealing a safe.

Kevin spun the wheel, entering the combination. It opened on the first try. He pulled out a stack of newly minted paper money, counted it, took what Rico owed and put the rest back.

Rico writhed on the chair, the sharp metal still stuck into him, blood leaking from the wounds. Vance felt sick just looking at him.

Kevin, satisfied, returned his attention to Rico. Nodded. Sapphire plucked out the blades as Rico winced.

"Call yourself an ambulance," Kevin said, pocketing the bloody stars. "We're done here."

"You damn freaks!" Rico screamed after them as the Kaiden exited.

Vance followed Kevin through the hallway, the other three Kaiden trailed behind. The bouncer had crawled off somewhere. Loud music greeted them as the show continued unabated.

As they spilled into the club, the crowd remained blissfully unaware of their presence. Their eyes remained locked on the spectacle on stage.

Vance felt numb, disassociated from the situation. He just wanted to get the hell out of there.

Movement. He turned. The bald bouncer lunged toward them, face flushed with equal parts terror and rage.

Vance stepped forward unleashed a series of strikes, then twisted, under-hooking the bouncer's shoulder, tossing him on his head.

The bouncer lay on the floor, unresponsive. Either knocked out or dead. Vance didn't care which.

Stepping over the bouncer, they trudged out of the club and into the night.

They flew off into a dark sky. The giddiness buzzing through all of them, except for Vance. Then Sapphire's demonic effigy smiled at him, and he couldn't help but smile back.

Vance's body felt good as he ascended the path to meet Kevin. The crispness of the air awoke his senses and cleared his mind. He tried not to think about last night, and pushed the emotions away, a bipolar gestalt of soaring highs and storm cloud lows.

At the top Kevin awaited him, his face stoic, a watchful teacher evaluating his student.

"This is your last training session in daylight," Kevin said as Vance trudged toward him. Vance's breathing only slightly elevated now that his lungs had become used to the exertion.

"You handled yourself fine last night," Kevin said, as if he could read Vance's mind. Maybe he could.

Kevin held up a thin sharp diamond-shaped metal plate from a stack wrapped in a black cloth.

"This is the hallmark of the ninja. The *senban shurikan* was commonly carried by carpenters and used as nail extractors. *Shinobi* sharpened and repurposed them as distraction weapons."

"Distraction weapons?" Vance asked, a little surprised. "They looked more dangerous when you threw them at Rico."

Kevin laughed. His voice sounded flat in the cool morning air.

"Despite what I used them for, the real technique is to bite into flesh without sticking into the target. That way, the enemy can't pull them out and throw them back at you."

"In the movies, they can kill."

"Hollywood loves to exaggerate. In ancient times, they were coated in rust. In a time before tetanus shots, a cut from one could cause infection resulting in a slow and agonizing death."

"Sounds nasty."

"I'm sure it was," Kevin said handing Vance a stack of nine sharpened sheet-metal stars. They felt cold in his hand. "Once you get good at throwing these, you'll find that you can throw anything with decent accuracy."

Kevin taught Vance the basics, instructing him to rock his knees for momentum, engaging his full body instead of flicking his wrist.

"Use the same arm movement to throw as with your inside to outside block," Kevin said.

They tossed the stars into a plywood target set up on the edge of the woods just in front of Vance's straw wrapped tree.

Over the next few nights, Sho and Kevin continued Vance's training.

Outside, in the woods at night, Kevin taught Vance to move quietly through the environment, how to scamper to mask his human movement and mimic the sounds of an animal. He also taught him how to hide his thoughts and intentions so that an unfocused mind would not betray him.

Vance crawled on his belly, careful to remain invisible by hugging the ground and minimizing vertical movement. The instruction included techniques for seeing through the darkness without technology, and how to camouflage himself in rural and urban settings.

Kevin showed Vance how to roll and drop to the ground, giving the appearance, in the darkness, of vanishing. Something that had only been explained to him in the dojo setting. Vance felt sure illusions like that helped to cement the image of the ninja as a demon capable of becoming invisible at will.

Then came the *shujenja* training of undergoing harsh endurance and fear inducing experiences to expand his ability to move without fear through the world.

Kevin held Vance's ankles in the darkness as he dangled over a cliff without a net. He heard only his rapid heartbeat and the darkness shrouded surf below.

Kevin had Vance walk over a sea of red-hot coals after teaching him the mind setting techniques of *kuji-in*, the fire beneath his feet feeling no worse than hot pavement on an August day.

When his mind was clear enough, Sho added sensitivity training to the mix, thrusting a training knife at the small of Vance's back until Vance's brain registered Sho's killing intention.

As Vance improved, he found his body automatically slipped to the side, avoiding the killing blow.

Each night, with the training completed, Kevin drove Vance to the secret apartment. Vance hung out with the Kaiden, enjoyed Sapphire's company, drank expensive champagne, and soared into the night on black wings.

"This is your final test, Mr. Palladian," Sho said, unsheathing his katana. "Sit in seiza with your back to me."

Vance did as instructed. He knelt on the tatami mats of the Teahouse Dojo with his back straight, his thighs spread apart, toes touching, his feet forming a triangle behind him. Vance gently placed his hands on his upper thighs. He felt a trickle of sweat from underneath his right arm.

Kevin stood off to the side like an expectant parent awaiting the delivery of a newborn child.

A clammy chill overcame him.

What the hell am I doing?

Vance's heart hammered. He forced himself to steady his breathing. He needed to focus his mind. It was a matter of life and death.

He had become very good at avoiding a training blade thrust at him from behind, but there was no turning back from this. Sho's resolve and adherence to the warrior way meant he was willing to kill his student in the initiation ceremony.

Now totally focused, his heart returning to a slow and steady rhythm, Vance felt a slight twitch and a desire to move.

Vance opened his eyes and realized he had traversed a nine-foot distance without realizing it. Space and time had contracted, and his body had rolled as it had been trained to do.

Sho stood poised, the sword tip pointing at the ground, an over commitment of the weapon that would have sliced right through Vance if he hadn't moved. Sho smiled, and the elation of the moment made the room seem brighter.

Kevin clapped softly and nodded his head, a smile brightening his face.

"I knew you were the one," Sho said. "So few students pass a test like this.

"You have exemplified the heart under the blade."

"Blade above heart?" Vance said, absently.

"Yes, the *kanji* for ninja means a man who is silent. But the kanji can also be read as blade above heart: one who can endure a life and death struggle, even when the odds are stacked against him."

"I think I'm ready to do what I came here for," Vance said.

"What do you think, Kevin?" Sho asked turning to look at his soon to be son-in-law. "Do you think he's ready?"

"He's completed the training," Kevin said. "I'll leave it up to you."

"Kevin is too kind. He doesn't want to make a decision that ultimately, he believes, should be mine. But when a father gives his daughter away, the responsibility rests on the husband."

"He's not married yet," Vance said, and winked at Kevin. Sho still had an old-world way of seeing things. As if he still lived at the beginning of the 20th century.

"Good enough, Mr. Palladian," Sho said. "I'll let you take on your duties. Come with me. I have something to show you."

Chapter Eleven

Keikan practiced traditional martial arts patterns with classical music in the background. Active meditation with Baroque helped him relax. He had moved his coffee table transforming his living room into a makeshift dojo.

He needed to complete his own routine, anyway. Teaching wasn't the same as training. Having the discipline to practice solo, to drill techniques over and over until it became part of his muscle memory, set him apart from the couch potatoes of the world. The synergy between mind and body held the key to incredible fighting prowess. When balance, positioning, tension, and relaxation all combined into the perfect mix.

Keikan slowly worked his classical martial arts patterns, extending his body and limbs, softly creating an isometric squeeze at the end of each movement to generate an internal power known as *Chi*, *Qi*, or *Ki*, depending on the land of origin.

The eastern world presented the concept as something supernatural, but Keikan's experiences had shown him that the seemingly preternatural abilities of some martial arts masters actually came from a heightened understanding of the physical as opposed to the spiritual. Although, he didn't deny the existence of the paranormal or the supernatural. He was intimately acquainted with it.

In the first stage Keikan had learned basic mechanics, allowing him to hone his body into a formidable weapon. Later, once power had been cultivated through correct body movement and alignment, he only had to hold these states of being in his mind to generate the same results.

A generic ring tone cut his training short. Maybe a telemarketer flagrantly disregarding the Do Not Call Registry or simply a wrong number. Not recognizing the number, he hesitated but answered anyway.

"Hey, detective," a woman said. A hint of sultriness, maybe a tinge of fear. "This is Star."

"Star?" Keikan asked. The name didn't connect.

"From the Dancing Hour," she said. Recognition. Her naked breasts popped into his mind. He pushed the image away along with the stirring in his groin.

"Oh, right! Star," Keikan said. "What's up? You in trouble?"

"You asked me to call you if anyone ever showed up in costume again. Thought it'd be worth something to you."

"Yeah, definitely," Keikan said. "What happened?"

"You'll want to talk to my boss. An ambulance is coming. Better make it quick."

Star ended the call.

Keikan raced through the streets of Providence, blue and white strobing lights from the Mazda's grill painting the surroundings in patches of light.

Pulling into the parking lot of The Dancing Hour, Keikan parked as close as possible to the entrance. He'd have to be quick if he was going to get any information out of the club owner.

An ambulance had pulled up by the entrance. EMTs wheeled out the proprietor on a stretcher. Keikan hurried toward them. As he approached, he flashed his badge.

"I need a word with the patient," Keikan said.

"We'll give you a moment," one EMT said. Her partner nodded and they walked toward the front of the ambulance to give him some privacy.

"Hey, I don't talk to cops," Rico said, his voice sounded strained.

"You don't want me to help you?" Keikan said.

"You can't help me," Rico said. "Hey, keep that asshole away from me!"

Keikan looked up. Hayden approached.

"Don't worry, I have him on a short leash," Keikan said, giving Hayden a look. Hayden nodded and walked away to cool his heals out of earshot.

Keikan had thought long and hard before asking Hayden to meet him at The Dancing Hour. Bringing him to the strip club might end up being a mistake. Hayden had written his most controversial books on The Dancing Hour slayings.

If the news media got wind of it, who knew where it could all go. He didn't like the idea of being featured on tabloid TV. Keikan also didn't want to cause a panic. He could see that happening if the public thought the killer had returned. Even with all his fears, Keikan couldn't leave his partner out of the loop. That would be a serious breach of trust. Hopefully, Hayden wouldn't do anything stupid.

"Looks like you fell on a bunch of knives," Keikan said, observing Rico's patched wounds. "Want to tell me who did this to you?"

"I know how to speak Spanish and English," Rico said. "I have no idea how to say fuck you in Chinese."

"It's Japanese," Keikan said.

"Look, like you said," Rico said. "I fell."

"They're going to keep doing this to you," Keikan said. "You can help me stop them."

"I ain't no snitch," Rico said, then clammed up.

Keikan caught the eye of an EMT. Nodded his head. As they returned, Keikan murmured his thanks and then approached Hayden.

"How's Rico?" Hayden asked.

"Somebody used him as a dartboard, but he won't talk."

"Figures," Hayden said. "What do you want to do now?"

"Close it down and interrogate everyone."

"Good move," Hayden said, nodding.

"Can I trust you to secure the scene while I do the interviews?" Keikan asked.

Hayden gave him a wink and walked off to get the yellow tape.

While Hayden cordoned off the area, Keikan looked for a location for the interviews. With the lewd posters pulled down, Rico's office would do nicely. The office smelled a smidge musty but nothing too off-putting.

He rearranged the chairs in the office to allow for a comfortable interview.

"Everyone's ready to go," Hayden said, peaking in.

"Thanks," Keikan said. "Write their names and stage names," Keikan said. "Make sure I meet with Star last. I want more time with her."

Keikan began his process with the male staff and customers, writing down whatever they noticed, which wasn't much. Then he worked through all the dancers.

After a long interview process, with little to show for it, he sat across from Star, forcing his eyes from her cleavage. Her skin was smooth and elastic, belying what must have been a hard life. Makeup hid any imperfections. She wore a little too much perfume.

"Two hundred," Star said, tapping the foot of her crossed leg in the air. "Up front."

"Two bills, eh?" Keikan said, pretending to consider the fee. He could expense the money from petty cash. Cops always listed these expenses as various. They didn't want to record that the money was going to an informant, especially a stripper.

He retrieved his wallet, counted the crisp twenties, and handed them to her.

"Know how much dry humping I have to do to make this much money?" Star asked as she snatched the cash.

He didn't answer, just shifted in his seat. She was trying to manipulate him sexually. It was working.

"I don't know how much info I can give you," Star said as she stuffed the bills into her ample cleavage, like some dame in a noir flick. So, cliché, Keikan thought. Yet so effective. He forced his mind back to the matter at hand. "Like I told you on the phone, they were wearing costumes... masks."

"What type of masks? Describe them."

"I don't know. They looked Chinese to me, Asian. You know? But ghoulish. Like demons. Bird-like. Professionally made, you know, like they had stepped off a movie set. Not like some shitty plastic Ben Cooper costume from a Party Center."

"How many?"

"How many what?"

"Masked bird-demons."

"I counted five," Star said.

"What about the new guy you mentioned?" Keikan asked.

"Athletic guy, around five-seven, give or take," Star said. "I got the feeling the others were showing him the ropes. He was white?"

"A white guy? How do you know?"

"I saw his hands."

Keikan pondered that for a bit. Then pulled out five more crisp twenty-dollar bills from his jacket pocket and handed it to her. "You've earned it."

"You certainly like to throw around money, Keikan," Star said. "Come by and see me sometime."

She got up to leave as Hayden opened the door.

"*Ciao*, Keikan," Star said, winking at him before brushing past Hayden. Keikan wondered how many venereal diseases he could catch from her. The world might never know.

Chapter Twelve

Vance looked up at a breathtaking night sky. He made his way down the hill with Sho and Kevin, enjoying the canopy of stars as they traveled. No clouds obscured the view. If not for the light pollution, Vance could have peered through the cosmos to the beginning of time itself.

They reached the carport. Entering, their footfalls echoed through the structure. The limo, along with a dozen other vehicles waited, some belonging to the staff, while others looked too expensive for a servant's salary.

"Bet you like fast cars," Sho said as he handed Vance a set of keys. "Any of my vehicles in the garage, except for the limo, are at your disposal."

Vance pressed the unlock button on the key fob.

A sleek black Corvette beeped and flashed its parking lights twice.

"I think this one suits your style."

"Damn right it does," Vance said, approaching the Corvette, unable to hide his smile.

"You don't need a car anymore," Kevin whispered to him.

Vance raised his eyebrows. He knew Kevin was playing with him. Transformation could only happen at night. Even then, flying wasn't always practical. Besides, he had other reasons to drive the car at night. Especially, if he had access to such a machine.

Then Sho's face darkened.

"We're missing a motorcycle," Sho said.

"Missing? What happened to it?"

"Jade took it," Kevin said. "She thinks we wouldn't notice."

"My mind isn't that gone," Sho said, looking past Vance wistfully as if searching for something lost forever. "At least, not yet. She stows it in the woods and when she becomes impetuous and bored, she goes for a ride."

"What she doesn't know is that all the vehicles have tracking devices installed," Kevin said handing him a palm sized electronic tracker. "Keep it with you at night. She only sneaks out after dark."

"Follow her and make sure she doesn't get into trouble," Sho said. "I really hate spying on her, but she should have learned her lesson the last time. Just keep her safe."

Vance nodded. He'd certainly do his best. He had a feeling Jade would do her best to thwart his efforts.

"But first," Sho said. "I have something to show you."

Back at the mansion, Sho brought Vance into a study lined with ceiling to floor bookshelves, furnished with a stately desk and a leather chair. Two human sized figures mounted on pedestals stood draped with white dust cloths. Vance and Sho had to walk by the one on the left to get to their respective sides of the desk. The other stood off to the right, closer to the bookshelves. Vance figured they must be marble statues, maybe even museum pieces, but they reminded him of mannequin bags used for solo training. Their appearance in low light made his skin crawl, the same as the one in Jax's private dojo.

What did Freud call it? Unheimlich?

Sho lifted a black suitcase and placed it on the desk.

"I've collected some items for you," Sho said as he opened the case. "Everything in here is the modern equivalent of ancient ninja equipment."

"First, the ninja had a *takuhatsugasa*, a wide and deep straw hat worn by traveling monks. Like any hat, it kept the sun and rain off their heads and out of their eyes. But for the ninja it also masked their appearance, allowing them to blend in. The modern equivalent is simply a pair of sunglasses and a ball cap."

Sho placed a dark blue hat and a set of shades on the desk.

"The ninja carried a *kagi* hook and *nawa* rope, a grappling hook. If you carried one today, you'd be arrested for possessing burglary tools. But that's just what it is, a tool. In this case, a tactical knife and Leatherman multi-tool will provide you with all the functionality you need.

"A stone pencil, the *sekihitsu*, would still work today, but you'll find it easier to carry an aluminum tactical pen with a small notebook.

"Kampo, field medicine, used to be for stomach ailments. Everything you need is in this small first aid kit.

"You'll also substitute the *tenugui*, cloth for a bandana and a parachute cord bracelet.

"Since *uchidake* would be used to start a fire to obtain heat and light, you'll find a windproof lighter and a tactical flashlight more useful."

"For your weapons, we might have to skirt the law a little. I will show you them next, but I want you to understand why I'm giving you all these implements. The concept is called *banpen fugyo*, 10,000 changes--and yet--no surprises!"

Vance understood. By carrying the right equipment, he'd always have everything he needed for any situation that might arise.

Later that night, the tracking device chirped, alerting Vance of Jade's movement across the estate. Either they had bugged her clothing or her handbag. That set off alarm bells. Sho and Kevin never mentioned bugging anything except the vehicles. He'd have to sweep all his stuff along with the cottage to make sure no one was keeping tabs on him.

He stood up from the couch and placed a battered dogeared hardback of *The Book of Five Rings* by Miyamoto Musashi he'd been reading back on the coffee table. Strategy and philosophy were just as important as physical technique.

He looked at his watch: *11 pm. Where the hell was she going at this time of night?*

Pulling the device from his front pocket, he studied the palm-sized tracker. She was headed for the gate.

She'd be using *shinobi aruki*, ninja stealth walking and goton *po*, the five-element escape method, to leave the compound unnoticed.

Despite Kevin telling him he didn't need to drive; he couldn't see transforming and going off after her in tengu form. Not only wasn't he comfortable enough to do that by himself, he figured he'd frighten her if she saw him like that. She hadn't been told about this part of the tradition, and Vance didn't feel it was his place to let her in on the secret.

Luckily, he had stayed dressed. He decided from now on he would have to remain at least partially clothed, even while sleeping. He might have to go after her on a moment's notice.

Kevin had taught him to wear dark blue or charcoal grey garments instead of black. Black clothing tended to create a silhouette that could be easily seen contrasting against buildings, the night sky, or a light source.

Tonight, he wore dark wash jeans roomy enough that he could still kick, a dark blue long-sleeve shirt, and a pair of grey running shoes.

He grabbed a dark brown leather bomber jacket and the gear Sho had given him, slipped out of the cottage, and out into the night.

Vance booked it to the carport. Flying would require him to remove his shirt and jacket.

When he arrived without breathing heavy, Vance knew he was making great progress on his cardio. He slid behind the wheel of the Corvette, started the engine.

The car suited him; lean, muscular, and powerful. Just like he was becoming.

At the end of the private drive the guard opened the gate. Vance pulled his vehicle out onto the road, speeding off to find Jade.

Where the hell could she be? Vance thought as he entered Providence. He felt sure Jade didn't know about Kevin's apartment or the Kaiden operation hiding within the Maramoto organization. The nightlife in Providence existed but it wasn't exceptional; at least as he remembered it. He had left his partying days behind him many years ago. Was he already becoming an old man?

He navigated the Corvette into a back lot flanked by rundown buildings. Glancing at the GPS location tracker, he could see she now traveled on foot. Yet, he couldn't see her motorcycle anywhere. He parked and shut the engine down.

Pocketing the keys, he got out of the car. Just in case, he removed his jacket and shirt, placing them in the back seat. The night air cooled his skin.

Why the hell was he walking around without a shirt on? If she asked, he'd just tell her he was overheated from exercising.

Vance held the tracking device as he walked through the parking area. Even though packed with vehicles, the lot felt abandoned.

Following the homing blip on the display screen, he found Jade's motorcycle abandoned halfway down an alley.

A flash of movement caught his attention. He looked up and saw Jade. She ran for the opening on the opposite side of the alley, her form backlit from the lights of the adjoining parking lot.

Vance took off in pursuit, utilizing silent running to keep from being discovered.

She exited the alley and disappeared out of site.

Jade's youth, and perhaps her dysfunctional family, drove her to self-destruction. Vance had done many things himself in his younger days he wasn't proud of and looking back he wondered how he had survived long enough to make it to adulthood.

Some adulthood! He had gone from teacher of karate kids, to playing ninja, to whatever he was doing now. He felt he was living in a dream. Was it really a nightmare?

"Hey girlie, what ya doing out here alone?" A male voice echoed through the alleyway.

Without thought, Vance transformed. He felt the change overcoming his humanity. Vance turned sideways to accommodate his wings as he flew though the cramped throughway, picking up speed, before lifting straight up.

Vance soared through the night on tenebrous wings. From high above, the streets and alleyways reminded him of a maze.

Jade was headed for more than a nightclub. From his vantage point, he could see she was headed for trouble.

"Why don't we all party?" a large man said. He wore black clothing with a knit cap to match. He licked his lips.

Vance swooped in behind her.

"Do you gentlemen have a problem?" Vance asked, emerging on foot from the darkness into the dimly lit parking lot. He knew Jade could take care of herself. Yet, Sho had charged him with being her protector. He had accepted. Therefore, he reasoned, he owned this fight.

Four men stood before Jade. The large man in the knit cap, an even larger man wearing a leather jacket, another, taller and thinner, who sported a white hoody, and a dude who wore his sunglasses at night, like the old '80s song said.

"Who the fuck are you?" Knit Cap asked before a spastic shake of the head. "What the fuck are you?"

Jade turned to look at him. Vance nodded. It was almost a bow.

The four men distracted; Jade dive-rolled diagonally past them. Returning to her feet, she made her escape toward the buildings that acted as a boundary line for the property. Her footfalls echoed in the distance until they faded into the night.

Garbage wafted in with a breeze from somewhere. An open dumpster, maybe?

Could he really beat four men? He hadn't at the Quick Mart. But things had changed. He had changed, in more than one way. All indecision fled.

"You must be crazy, man," White Hoody said. "Who are you, Big Bird?"

"Yeah," a bigger man in a leather jacket said. "Take off that costume."

"I'm not wearing a costume," Vance said. "This is who I really am."

"I'm gonna cut that mother fucking suit off you," Hoody said, flicking open a switchblade.

"Not a good idea, friend," Vance said.

He meant it, every word, and he tried to project those intentions, bad intentions, to the four would be attackers. He didn't feel fear, and society's stranglehold on him, the morals and ethics that kept him from killing had vanished.

They continued to advance, but a hint of dread colored their eyes.

Leather Jacket pounced. Vance avoided the attack, stomping diagonally through Leather's leg, breaking bone, and cartilage. Vance felt nothing. No sympathy. No remorse. Leather screamed as he flopped onto the pavement.

Big Man lunge-punched. Vance snatched his wrist midair and twisted it, circling inside, completing the throw. His face smashed into unforgiving concrete. A terrible sight: blood, torn flesh, and dislodged teeth. Either unconscious or dead, Big Man no longer moved.

Vance flicked his wrist, letting loose sharpened throwing stars that had been stowed in his pants pocket. His aim was true. They found their mark, puncturing Knit Cap's torso, arms, and face. Knit Cap stumbled and fell to the ground, grunting.

The man in the hoody flailed, slashing blindly with the switchblade. Vance snatched Hoody's arm, yanking him off balance. Vance hit the blunt top of the blade, disarming, and lobbing the knife back and into him. Grabbing the knife and twisting, he listened to a symphony of screams.

Sunglasses, mouth agape, removed his namesake and let them drop to the pavement before running for his life. Vance thought about pursuing but since he was going in the opposite direction from Jade, he let the former sunglass man go.

Not caring if his attackers lived or died, he flew off to find Jade and get away before the police and media arrived.

Chapter Thirteen

"I only have a knife," Keikan said, showing the training blade to his self-defense class of law enforcement officers that had filed into the situation room turned dojo. "Lt. Love, if you would do me the honor."

Detective John Gray took his mark in front of him. While climbing the ranks, Gray had garnered the nickname Lieutenant Love. His namesake, an author, had written relationship books about men and women being from different planets.

Keikan paced out approximately twenty feet, then turned around to face him. The rest of the class framed the training area.

"Do you feel safe?" Keikan asked.

"I guess I shouldn't," Love said. "But at this distance, seeing you only have a knife, I'm pretty confident."

"See how that works for you," Keikan said. "As soon as I make my move, draw your weapon and fire. This is only make-believe. I don't want to get shot and leave you guys to clean up the mess."

The class laughed nervously. They all wore their duty blues except for Keikan who wore a black t-shirt with matching training pants.

Keikan waited. Allowed the tension between them to become palatable. Then he tensed his muscles and exploded into a run.

Love stumbled back, trying to draw the training pistol.

Keikan reached him in microseconds, slashing and stabbing, the training blade leaving lipstick lines across Love's uniform to simulate wounds.

Love just shook his head and laughed softly. The others laughed as well, releasing tension. Keikan returned his attention to the loose formation of students.

"This is a Tueller drill," Keikan said.

Created by Salt Lake City Police Sergeant, Dennis Tueller and first published in an article titled "How Close is Too Close" in a 1983 issue of SWAT magazine, the drill showed how easy it was to be bested by a perp armed with only a knife.

"Let's switch roles."

Keikan gave Love his training knife and tightened Love's duty belt around his own waist.

Keikan took a deep breath, cleared his mind. He didn't want to lose face in front of the other officers.

Love rushed him.

Keikan waited, slowing his breathing to keep his body under control.

He didn't make a move for his pistol. Instead, at the last second, he stepped diagonally into a pocket of safe space away from the blade. Turning, he grabbed Love's weapon hand, using momentum and physics to flip Love onto his back.

Love grunted and hit the floor, stomping his feet to dissipate the force of the throw. Ukemi.

Controlling Love's arm, Keikan used his knee as a fulcrum to turn Love onto his stomach. Once pinned, Keikan disarmed him, stowed the knife in the duty belt, and then drew his simulated weapon, training it on Love.

"See? Simple?" Keikan said with a wink. "Do that."

The class laughed again, picked partners, and went at it. Rhythmic thuds of students hitting the floor filled the air. Keikan went around giving pointers until time ran out.

"Okay, let's call it a night," Keikan said, dismissing the class. "Next time, we'll be back to Kendo training. Don't forget your sword and armor."

After the class had filed out, Keikan met with the group that hung back.

"Finnegan, I think you've met Love," Keikan said. Finnegan nodded.

Then Keikan introduced Officer Puja Patel-Morran, her lustrous black hair tied in a bun. A smaller woman, she knew how to make her size an advantage.

Finnegan introduced Officer Jamal Anderson, an African American man who looked like he spent all his spare time in the weight room. What Anderson lacked in flexibility and mobility he sure made up for with intimidation and strength.

Keikan let them know his plan. They were all game. Keikan had his team.

George Hayden entered the hall.

"You're too late to train," Keikan said, straight-faced, but he couldn't keep up the charade and he pursed his lips to stifle a smile.

"Yeah, yeah," George said, waving off the joke.

The team dispersed, nodding their goodbyes, but Keikan could feel an animosity directed toward Hayden. If Hayden felt it, he didn't let it show.

"Why aren't you at home?" Keikan asked. "Thought you were going to spend a nice quiet evening with the missus."

"The description of our masked man came over the scanner. He did a number on four criminals. First responders found some exotic martial arts weapons. Chinese stars or some such. I called ahead and told them we'd be on the way."

"Has the ACD been alerted?" Keikan asked.

The State Police Asian Crimes Division was a natural next step for Keikan's career, even though Rhode Island didn't have a large Japanese population. Asian gang crime came mainly from Cambodians, Laotians, and even some Chinese closer to the shore. The division had become busier in 2009 when prostitution became illegal again. Unbeknownst to many out-of-staters, in 1980 a loophole made the oldest profession legal in the Ocean State.

Although his ethnicity made him a shoo-in for a state job, he wasn't sure he wanted to spend his career busting hookers. If things turned sour with the Chief, at least he had an exit strategy.

"Not yet," Hayden said, cocking his head.

"Don't call them. We'll handle it," Keikan said.

Keikan and Hayden arrived in the parking area where strobing lights from two ambulances, a fire rescue, and a patrol car fought a perpetual battle with the darkness.

EMTs flushed out the victim's eyes with saline, strapped them onto stretchers, worked to stop bleeding, and stabilized broken bones.

"Glad you got here," a stocky EMT said. "Can't wait much longer to transport these guys to the hospital. Cops are already making a report."

The EMT thumbed at two cops standing by their cruiser. One filled out paperwork while another finished his coffee. Keikan nodded, and they nodded back.

"What happened?" Keikan asked the EMT.

"Talk to this guy," he said, pointing at a young man wearing a knit cap, sitting on the back of a standard Type II ambulance. The man had blood-shot eyes and wore a bandage on his cheek. He clung to a blanket draped around his shoulders.

"I'll tell you what happened, man," Knit Cap said. "Same thing I told the other cops. This guy in a Halloween costume comes out of nowhere, and for no reason whooped our asses."

"What did the costume look like?" Hayden asked.

"A bird demon," the victim said. "Like something from Kabuki Theater or a Kung-Fu flick."

"How did he attack you?" Keikan asked.

"With ninja stars, man." Knit Cap said. "Can you believe it?"

"Where are the stars now?" Keikan asked.

"Police took them," Knit Cap said. Then his face brightened. "Hey, you think I could get them back? Keep 'em. You know, like a souvenir."

"I doubt it," Hayden said, shaking his head. "Wait here."

Hayden approached the patrol car and spoke with the cops for a second. Coffee Cop handed him an evidence bag.

As Hayden walked back, Keikan met him halfway.

"These are Chinese stars, aren't they?" Hayden asked when he returned.

"They haven't called them that since the '80s," Keikan said. "They're Japanese. *Senban Shurikan*. The real deal."

"What does that tell us?" Hayden asked.

"We have our first physical link to a Japanese martial arts master, and it's not a huge leap to find a tenuous connection to Sho," Keikan said.

"Circumstantial," Hayden said.

"We also know that he has a new person working for him—an amateur."

"How do you know that?" Hayden asked.

"Whoever turned Rico into a dartboard didn't leave any evidence," Keikan said. "Whoever threw the stars didn't bother removing them. He's careless, and every time he slips, we'll get one step closer to him."

"So, what's next?" Hayden asked.

"We find him."

Chapter Fourteen

The abandoned warehouse cleaned up and turned into an underground rave club, packed with writhing bodies. The sickly-sweet smell of marijuana, and the musk of perfume, cologne, sweat, and body odor all intermingled, assaulting the senses. So distracted were they by euphoria, electronica, and Ecstasy, Vance slipped through the crowd unnoticed.

Loud music pummeled his eardrums. How would he find her here? Jade had eluded him, had vanished like the Shinobi of legend.

Then, just as he had given up hope, he saw her on the second-floor balcony. Could that really be her? Maybe Ecstasy had entered his system, some sort of contact high or shared communal hallucination.

One last push through the revelers and he reached the staircase. Ascended. Reaching the mezzanine, Jade was nowhere to be found.

He felt eyes upon him. Vance whirled to face whoever watched him from below.

Chapter Fifteen

"When you said we were going to look for him," Hayden said, out of breath, trying to keep up. " I didn't think you meant tonight."

Keikan hushed him. He needed to listen. The parking lots were filled. Something was going down, and he doubted it was legal.

"You hear that?" Keikan asked Hayden.

"Hear what?" Hayden said, huffing and puffing.

"Never mind," Keikan said, pointing. "Keep walking. Wait for me outside the building with the loud music."

"What building…?"

Keikan sprinted toward the music. He didn't care if Hayden caught up or not.

The structure wasn't hard to find. The bouncer sprawled on the ground was the only sign he needed, along with the pounding base.

Keikan felt for a pulse. Slow and rhythmic. Unconscious but not dead.

A wall of sound hit him when he entered the underground club. He waded into the crowd unnoticed. A blur on the mezzanine caught his eye. A demon stood on the indoor balcony, his back to the revelers below.

The tengu felt his stare. The creature spun around.

A hand touched Keikan's shoulder. Startled, he whipped around. Hayden. He'd finally arrived. Exertion had drained his face of color.

Keikan whirled toward the mezzanine. The balcony stood empty. The tengu had vanished.

Chapter Sixteen

"Where've you been?" Kevin asked, as Vance got out of the car. His voice sounded distant, swallowed by the night, and hollowed out by the carport. He leaned against the limo with arms crossed and an unreadable expression.

"Keeping your fiancée out of trouble," Vance said.

Kevin smiled.

"What this time?"

"Dancing at an underground club," Vance said. Kevin's expression turned sour. "Don't worry, she's safe. I don't think she'll sneak out again for a while."

"How can you be sure?" Kevin asked.

Vance pointed at the bike.

"She put the bike back where it belongs," Vance said. "Let's hope it stays there."

"I'm glad you were there for her," Kevin said, then he shifted gears. "The Kaiden has another visit to make. I didn't want to leave without you."

Vance didn't care about the people inside the club. The barriers of morality, his super-ego, crumbled slowly until only his ego and Id remained. Without pesky ethics, Vance could escape into a world without consequence, a world of violence and, if he were lucky, maybe even a little sex.

This time, he did the honors of approaching the doorman. No shirt. No shoes. No service. When the doorman protested and barred them from entering, Vance transformed. The burley bouncer let out a cry and then turned on his heels to flee. Vance was upon him too quickly. Then they were airborne. Vance snaked a well-trained arm around the bouncer's throat and applied pressure with the other hand to create a standing, or in this case, flying variant of the *sankaku jime*, triangle choke. In less than a minute, the bouncer slumped—unconscious.

Vance landed and let him drop to the ground.

"After you," Vance said to the Kaiden. He would give them deference. After all, he was extra muscle, not the leader. That was Kevin's job. Like any good soldier, Vance would await orders.

Vance followed the Kaiden as they transformed into tengu and weaved their way around the VIP tables, set up for the wealthier patrons to enjoy the show with never ending glasses of expensive champagne. Above and to the side, spectators on bleachers screamed for blood. To the right, they had erected an octagon fighting cage. Inside, two pugilists beat each other in an unsanctioned rule-less version of Mixed Martial Arts. They threw down sans safety equipment. Much blood flowed.

Kevin made his way toward a table nestled in a shadowy corner of the makeshift amphitheater. The lowlight hid their tengu features and the spectacle kept the audience distracted.

Two burley strong-jawed thugs stepped in front of Kevin.

Two men, both dressed in black suits, each groping an equally big-breasted ring girl, sat behind the table. One man, pockmarked face, hair greasy, waved off the muscle and shooed away the silicon-enhanced bimbos.

"Have a seat, freaks," the ugly guy said, pointing to an empty chair across from him. "This is MMA, not the WWE."

"You're hilarious," Kevin said, taking a seat.

Vance noted muscle off to the side, a few more cooling their heels in the crowd. They all looked the same, as if pressed out of a mold in a bodyguard factory.

Vance noticed a lit utility closet with the door ajar. About a dozen Louisville Sluggers leaned against the inside wall—cheap insurance against a riot.

"My freaky friend," the ugly man continued. "This is not the best time."

"Not the best time," the other ugly man said, shaking his head.

"We're the only reason you haven't been shut or shaken down. Without our protection, you'll be eaten by wolves."

"What the fuck? You threatening me? In my club?" the gangster said. "Fuck you. Get the fuck out of here. You give me no respect."

"Yeah, where's your respect?" the other man asked.

The bodyguards inching close, joined by two jacked up martial artists. Their ears battered from a lifetime of fighting. Cauliflower city.

Vance slipped into the shadows. Unnoticed. He reached the closet, grabbed an armful of baseball bats.

He tossed one to each of the Kaiden, except for Kevin, who remained seated. Vance kept one for himself.

The Ninth God wrapped his big mitts around polished wood and took to the air.

Chaos as the Kaiden flew around on a bludgeoning spree, hitting anyone who got in their way, blood and teeth spitting through the air. Each thwack of the bat, the impact of hardwood on equally hard bone, thrilled and satisfied him in an ancient and visceral way.

Screams in the crowd as some noticed, but not enough to create a panic.

"What the fuck are you doing?" Kevin asked, suddenly hovering beside him, stopping him from another satisfying swing. The MMA fighter he just hit teetered in a delayed reaction before dropping to the floor.

Kevin's tengu face flushed with anger. "You never give my guys bats. I don't let them carry weapons for a reason."

Kevin drew a pistol. He pointed the gun at the ceiling and squeezed the trigger. A sharp blast that made Vance's ears ring. An overhead light exploded. Glass shattered. Shards rained down. A puff of smoke hung in the air.

Cheers turned to screams as panic overtook the crowd. They trampled each other as they made for the exit.

The Kaiden dispersed, flying into the shadows and out into the night.

"The goal is to make money, not to destroy the business," Kevin said once they'd assembled outside.

Vance nodded. Kevin was right. His rashness might have destroyed this prospect. He needed to stop listening to the devil nestling on his shoulder.

Then the Ninth God gave him a wink, and Sapphire nodded. The Golden Dragon couldn't contain his laughter. None of them could, even Kevin. They laughed like escapees from a lunatic asylum before taking to the sky.

Chapter Seventeen

Lieutenant Love stood post outside the underground fight club, a kaleidoscope of light bathing him in Technicolor.

"Thought you might be interested in this," Love said, looking at Keikan. "Reports of costumed men. Some even say they were flying."

"Flying, huh? Probably too many hallucinogens. Otherwise, sounds like our guys," Keikan said. "I'll help process the scene. Let me send Hayden on his way."

Love hated Hayden. He had to keep them separated for the time being. If his plan was going to work, he needed both of them.

Keikan returned to the Vic and talked to Hayden through the open window.

"What's our next move?" Hayden asked, drumming his thumbs on the wheel.

"We've been reactive. Time to go proactive," Keikan said.

"Meaning what?"

Keikan told him.

"You've got to be kidding," Hayden said, his jowls dropping.

"Get your affairs in order. We're in for some long evenings."

"Great," Hayden said, raising the power window. He drove off into the night.

Only a matter of time before he had Sho—and with Sho—Jade. She was the reason for doing this. Hayden would have to remain in the dark.

The day was quickly approaching. He just needed patience. He would pray for it tonight, as he did every night.

Chapter Eighteen

The next night, the Kaiden assembled at the apartment. Sapphire sat next to Vance on the couch. Even her radiant warmth couldn't take the chill from his bones. He had hoped they'd have spent the night drinking expensive wine and reconnecting as a team. He felt bad about messing up at the MMA joint. Yet, it seemed only Kevin had been miffed and his initial anger was soon forgotten. Unfortunately, the wine would have to wait.

"A man who went by the warrior name Tiki left our organization," Kevin said.

"He was part of the Kaiden?" Vance asked, feeling hopeful. Maybe, after he was sure Jade was safe, there'd be a way out of all this. If this Tiki guy left, wouldn't it stand to reason that Vance could as well?

"Yes, a very trusted member," Kevin said.

"So, why is he out?" Vance asked.

"He stole contacts," Golden Dragon said. "Set up a lucrative drug ring. Became our competition."

"Drugs?" Vance asked. A knot tightening in his stomach.

Jax looked away. Remained silent.

"I don't like it any more than you," Kevin said, his voice compassionate. But his tone seemed discordant, disingenuous. " None of us do. But drug money is big money. Real money. We've only carved out a small business in the Ocean State. The Chinese control the bulk. We have to be careful. Get too greedy and we'll start a war. Last thing we want is war with the *Tongs*."

Vance had heard of the Tongs, a Chinese secret society in the United States that profiteered through organized crime. Yet, most of what he knew of them came from movies and TV.

"That's the biggest problem," Sapphire said. "If Tiki causes problems with the Tongs, they'll come after us."

"If we don't retaliate, we'll be seen as weak," the Ninth God said.

"So, what are we going to do?" Vance asked.

"Create mayhem and chaos," Sapphire said, flashing him a sly grin.

Vance and the Kaiden descended into an alleyway half a block from the warehouse. The stench of refuse lingered.

Adrenaline surged through Vance's system, preparing him to fight.

Kevin handed each tengu a sheathed wakizashi from a stack stowed in a bag. The blade was as strong as its katana counterpart, but shorter and more maneuverable in close quarters battle. Each sword handle was hand wrapped in colorful silk.

"Thought you didn't allow your people to go in armed?" Vance asked, taking his sword. The weight of the Katana felt good in his hand.

"There's no profit in this business. Our blades won't hurt the cocaine."

With that, Kevin flew into the shadows, the others following. Vance hesitated, but only for a moment. He took off after them, prepared for war.

Chapter Nineteen

Jiro hated his position in the warehouse. Hated the monotony. The tons of cocaine he accepted weekly, a good portion ending up in the noses of American teenagers, didn't bother him.

What did bother him was being placed in charge of the third shift. Guarding the building was a no brainier. Reinforced steel covered the doors and windows. Plenty of guards roamed the facility, enough men to run a lucrative poker game.

After months of boredom, Jiro let the guys play to stay awake. He played to stay awake. Working the graveyard shift wreaked havoc with his circadian rhythm.

Worst of all, Jiro hated the dark. He hated arriving to work in darkness and leaving in the half-light. He usually stayed up the whole morning fighting the need for sleep, trying to complete normal chores and errands.

The money helped ease his suffering. He made more than enough to keep his wife at home caring for their two sons. Although, the arrangement was both a blessing and a curse. Especially when he needed some shuteye. She always had one more request for him.

Now he sat at the card table, nursing a beer, and holding onto his luck: a royal flush, the red of the hearts suit fanned out in his hands.

He planned to go home with some extra spending cash the Missus wouldn't know about. Maybe even sneak out to one of Rhode Island's ubiquitous strip bars where the girls flashed flesh while he inhaled secondhand smoke and imbibed watered-down drinks.

He pounded the table with his fist, unable to contain a smile.

"Read 'em and weep!" he said, placing the cards on the table. A guard groaned.

The lights went out.

"Fuck," Jiro heard himself say. He also heard expletives and the scraping of chairs, but he couldn't see a damn thing. Breaking into a sweat, his finger franticly searched for his night-vision goggles.

Someone screamed. One of his men? He couldn't tell. Where the hell were the goggles?

The swish of blades.

More screams.

The metallic smell of blood.

The deafening report of a sidearm.

A muzzle flash.

The light lasted long enough for Jiro to see his goggles on the floor. Pulse pounding, he dove.

Now prone, he secured the goggles over his eyes. The cool rubber of the eye cups creating suction.

Flipping the switch, the night-vision activated with a whine.

His team, surrounded by *tengu*—by human sized crow demons! The green of the image intensification cast their demonic visages in a ghastly glow.

Tengu overwhelmed armed guards with nothing but antique swords. The thought threatened his sanity.

Of course, they didn't carry guns—they were demons of vengeance from old world Japan. They didn't need guns.

A tengu demon disarmed a guard, slicing through his wrist with his sword. The guard screamed. Blood spurted green across Jiro's vision. The gun clattered to the floor.

A female demon tore a guard apart with her claws. Each pass ripped off chunks of flesh and sent green splatter into the air.

That's when Jiro pissed his pants. His mind barely registering the wetness and the warmth.

Through the chaos, Jiro could only think of his sons. How they'd grow up without a father. No one to steer them away from the terrible cocaine shipments that would tempt them in high school. Would they abuse the products he helped perpetuate? What if they learned what he did for a living? Would they hate him or follow in his footsteps? The sins of the father, and all that.

He shook away the dark thoughts threatening to consume him.

Somehow, he had the presence of mind to crawl to the far wall where he could reach one of Tiki's swords that had been hung as a reminder of their shared Japanese warrior heritage.

Had Tiki known this would happen? Had he kept the katana within reach for just this moment when demons arrived, and a firearm would have no effect? If anything could kill these monsters, it was a katana, imported illegally from Japan, one deployed during the *Tokugawa shogunate.*

Jiro stood and steeled himself for combat.

Screaming, he raised his weapon in the *Jodan* upper posture, and charged their queen.

The she-demon whirled to meet his blade. Catching it with her bare hands—claws! At that moment, Jiro prepared to lose his mind before meeting his end.

Then the lights snapped on, destroying his vision. His sword was wrested from his grip.

The queen tore off his goggles, claws constricting his throat. Impact as she slammed him against the wall.

"I have a message for your boss," another demon growled in the shadows. "Understand?"

He tried to speak but couldn't get the words out. Instead, he nodded, barely. Suffocating, blackness bleeding into his vision.

"Good. Tell Tiki to stop doing business in Rhode Island. If not, he dies, you die, your families die. Everybody dies. Everybody!"

Jiro attempted to nod, but the world was slipping away.

Then the demonic queen let go. He slumped to the floor, grabbing his tender throat, coughing uncontrollably.

When he could breathe again, his dead comrades lay in pools of blood around him.

"Go!" the female demon growled.

Terror flooding through him, Jiro burst from the building and into the cool night.

He jumped into his Volvo and sped away. Tiki would get the message, but not in person. He'd send a letter. Snail-mail. Quaint. It would give Jiro time to get his family out of Dodge, escape to the West Coast, where Tiki didn't have the resources to find them. He swore to God he'd go straight this time. He hoped he wasn't lying to himself.

Chapter Twenty

V ance stood, chest heaving, sword and clothing covered in blood. He felt tired but wired. All his senses heightened.

A young Japanese American guard at his feet, cut down in the prime of his life. A .45 revolver lay in his slack hand.

The guard's eyes fluttered open.

He grasped the weapon, raised it.

Squeezed the trigger.

The blast deafening, Vance lifted his sword.

The blade severed the gunman's wrist. The guard's hand fell to the floor, death-gripping the gun.

The guard screamed, grasped his severed limb that spurted blood with each heartbeat and passed out.

Vance turned away from the gruesome aftermath and saw the damage already done.

Sapphire, her eyes ablaze with a mixture of rage and despair, kneeling, held Kevin in her arms, blood saturating his chest as he automatically transformed from demon to man.

The Golden Dragon and the Ninth God rushed to help, but it was no use. For Kevin, it was over.

Vance couldn't sleep. He couldn't believe Kevin was dead. Didn't want to believe it. The aftermath ran through his mind.

The Golden Dragon and The Ninth God had carried Kevin. They flew in silence, tears streaking Sapphire's face. They had lost everything that night. Nothing would be the same again. He couldn't imagine telling Sho… or Jade.

"You should have made sure the sentry was dead," the Ninth God finally said, breaking the mournful silence, his voice tight. Vance hadn't killed anyone, yet. At least as far as he knew. He had at least never killed anyone intentionally and he didn't plan to do so then or now. That was a step too far over the line.

"It's not his fault," Sapphire said, her voice cracking. "It's not anyone's fault. Kevin knew the risks."

"Bullshit," the Ninth God said. "This is the second time he screwed up. He's not one of us."

All the goodwill Vance had gained by giving Jax a baseball bat had vanished.

As the Ninth God's fury rose, Vance felt fortunate to be flying next to Sapphire. Vance couldn't blame Jax for being angry. He was the one who had failed, failed the Kaiden, Sho, Jade, and most of all—Kevin.

"You were never with us," Sapphire said, descending with him to the cottage.

Sapphire looked back before speeding off after the others. Vance had stood in silence, with nothing but dark thoughts and emotions.

Now, instead of sleeping, he paced the cramped living area. Then he knew what to do.

Vance stripped off his bloodied pants and wadded them up in a ball. He changed into shorts and got some items from under the kitchen sink.

Out back, Vance found a charcoal grill. He stuffed the jeans inside and doused it with lighter fluid.

Tossing in a lit match, he shielded his face with his arm as the fire flared. The blast of heat singed the air but could not warm him.

He watched the flames, comforted by the heat, until they had consumed everything.

The memory faded and he poured a glass of bourbon. He sipped, trying not to think, allowing the alcohol to act as anesthesia.

Finally, exhausted, he dropped into bed and fell into a deep and troubled sleep.

Chapter Twenty-One

Two weeks had elapsed as slowly as any stretch of time in Vance's life. In the mornings he had kept to his routine, early runs, basic striking against the tree, as if Kevin were still alive.

In the evening, with nothing much to do other than stew on his negative emotions, he'd pace and await a troubled sleep. And if sleep wouldn't come —pray for daylight.

The weird nights soaring over treetops and the city faded until they felt like a dream. The imaginings of a madman.

Finally, he received a message from Sho in the form of a note. An envelope had been taped to the outside door. At the appointed time, he left the cottage and made his way up the hill toward the mansion. No one greeted him or stopped him. His footfalls echoed through the halls announcing his presence until he reached Sho's study.

Sho sat behind his desk. The room creeped him out. Uncanny statues looked as if they might animate under their coverings, and old tomes lining built-in bookcases gave the impression of an evil wizard's lair. Sho sat sentinel to his ancient grimoires and lost arcanum.

"I'm sorry I didn't inform you of Kevin's death personally," Sho said, not bothering to look up from his ledgers.

"It's understandable," Vance said as he sat down across from Sho. The less he said, the less he had to lie. "I'm sorry for your loss, and for Jade. I've been training on my own to pass the time."

"Good. Very good," Sho said. His eyes looked distant, as if Kevin's death had robbed him of any remaining vitality.

"How's Jade?" Vance asked.

"As well as one can expect," Sho said. "Between the death and being cooped up behind the estate walls, she's going stir crazy. I fear she'll return to sneaking out at night. I'd like you to accompany her today on a shopping trip."

"Of course," Vance said, then added, "I'll need some info on her brother."

"I don't want to talk about him. You have the skills to keep her safe."

"I appreciate your faith in me...."

"You must understand how painful it is, especially after Kevin's death, to speak of my son."

Vance relented. The lines on Sho's face, usually hidden by good genes, riddled his expression, tracings of anguish scrawled over his aging skin.

Yet, without more information on Kudaki, Vance would remain in the dark about whereabouts and capabilities.

Worse, he had no experience with body guarding. The training that Sho and Kevin had given him, although top notch for combat, didn't take the realities of executive protection into account.

Keeping Jade safe had nothing to do with martial arts or weaponry. Executive and VIP protection had everything to do with pre-planning and risk mitigation.

To protect her, he'd need real world solutions, not the fighting arts of 1600s Japan. At the very least, he'd need research and recon. He couldn't transform into a tengu until after dark, and he wasn't even sure it was possible for him to do so anymore. Computer access and Jade's itinerary would be a start. Sho wasn't having it.

"You won't be able to pin down Jade that easily," Sho said. "I'll see if I can get you Internet access. My generation did everything the old-fashioned way."

"What are you doing here?" Jade asked as she approached.

Vance leaned against the limo parked outside the mansion. He had the distinct impression she feigned aggravation. Vance couldn't believe Sho hadn't told her he was coming.

"Your father thinks I should tag along." He could play the game.

"Wonderful," she said, pushing a pair of sunglasses over her nose.

Vance opened the door, and she slid to the opposite seat. With a Glencairn glass in hand, she poured a dram of eighteen-year-old single malt scotch, neat.

"It's not even noon, yet," Vance said, climbing in. He nodded to the driver, a young Asian male. With his cap on, the resemblance to Kevin was uncanny.

"Who are you, my father?" Jade asked, looking over her shades. Apathy dulled her eyes. Those eyes still captivated him.

She was right, he wasn't her father. He hadn't been hired to curtail her behavior, just keep her safe from physical threats. Let Sho deal with her drinking. Jade had weathered an enormous tragedy. He could certainly understand why she felt the need to drink. A nightcap or two had become de rigueur every evening since Kevin's death. He would have loved to have one but had to keep his wits about him and his senses alert.

"So, where are we going?" Vance asked, dropping the subject.

"Shopping," Jade said, taking a sip.

"Downtown, ma'am?" the driver asked.

She nodded, and they were off.

Jade sipped her drink and lost herself in her smartphone.

Vance returned to the task at hand, staying alert and in the moment.

As they left the estate, Vance noticed an early model sedan parked on the other side of the street. Back in the day, they used Crown Vic's as police cruisers.

The vehicle sat well enough back that he couldn't see any occupants. The vehicle didn't pursue them, but he made a mental note to look for that car again.

In stop and go traffic, Vance couldn't tell one vehicle from another. Which were benign? Which were potential threats? He did not know. He could be making mistakes and never realize it until it was too late.

Finally, they reached downtown Newport with its narrow cobblestone roads, whitewashed colonial buildings pressed into service as shops, squeezed in accordion style one on top of the other, and throngs of day-tripping tourists. The stars and stripes displayed outside many a building, waving brilliantly in the salty air.

Out here in the idyllic costal town, trouble waited. He felt it, and Vance didn't feel equipped to face it.

Chapter Twenty-Two

Keikan and Hayden waited on the side of the road. They had a clear view of the entrance to Sho's estate. A thicket of trees on either side hid the property from view, and the road itself eventually snaked off to the west, becoming scenic, the brilliance of the sun glinting off the choppy waters of Narragansett Bay. The air continued to warm, and summer was not long off.

This was no way to do an investigation, but Keikan felt it was his only option. He had to stakeout Sho's estate day and night, hitting different times, staying as long as they could stand.

Keikan was already sick of peeing in mason jars. Yet, he knew if they waited, they'd eventually catch a break. That was all he needed. Just one small little break.

One chance was all they'd be afforded, and if they screwed it up (most likely by Hayden) they'd be out of luck.

One false step and the police chief would have a grip on his junk so tight he could give up police work and play Frankie Valli in a revival of Jersey Boys.

"This isn't working, Chris," Hayden said, and then sighed. Hayden's attitude didn't help. He was the type of investigator who always wanted to be on the move. Keikan had learned the value of stillness, of waiting until just the right moment to spring on his prey.

"Give it time," Keikan said, trying to push the annoyance from his voice. "At least we're out of sight, out of mind."

They waited an hour more in silence. Keikan contemplated taking a pee. He figured as soon as they had filled up their mason jars they'd have to call it quits.

Finally, a limo emerged from the estate, pulled onto the road, and headed in the opposite direction. Hopefully, they hadn't been made.

Keikan didn't have to alert Hayden, he had already started his vehicle, surprisingly calm. Then Hayden eased the Vic onto the road, merging into to traffic to take up the chase.

Chapter Twenty-Three

Kevin's doppelgänger brought the limo to a stop in front of Gorflands boutique, as if he knew her needs and tastes telepathically.

Without waiting for assistance, Jade opened the limo door and stepped out onto the sidewalk. Vance followed suit. As he stepped out onto the sidewalk, Jade looked at him over her glasses before pushing them higher on her nose.

"I'll find a space around back," the driver said, tossing out a cell phone. Vance caught it and nodded. "Press Limo-1 when you need transport."

Vance didn't like the idea of the driver traipsing off, but signs prohibited parking on the street. If trouble found them, there was no way to quickly whisk Jade away to safety.

The limo pulled away.

"Stay outside," Jade said, as if scolding a guard dog. He opened his mouth to protest, but then thought better of it.

"It's a one room shop. You can easily see through the window. I don't need you in my way while I'm trying to relax," Jade said as if reading his mind.

Jade slipped into the shop, welcome bells tolling her arrival.

Downtown Newport elicited words like quaint or picturesque. Shopping trips and antiquing also came to mind. Not really his thing, but he couldn't deny the peaceful soundings, combined with the salt air, relaxed him. He imagined enjoying poking around the shops with a lady friend if the excursion ended with fish and chips, and especially a beer. Maybe two.

Surveying the area, he cooled his heels, kept watch, donned sunglasses when he tired of squinting at the sun.

Tourists strolled, and cars lolled through the sleepy seaside community.

An early model Crown Vic rolled up. Vance recognized it from its earlier parking spot outside the estate. The guy in the driver's seat wore an out-of-date mustache. His gray sport coat probably hid a shoulder holster. His age suggested he concealed a revolver. Maybe an old S&W Chief's .38 Special. That weapon choice would certainly suit an old school cop.

An Asian male, much younger than the older guy, exited the passenger side. His sport coat, a shade lighter, the material and the cut still in style, most likely hid a semi-auto. Probably a Glock. Vance wondered what they wore for backups on their ankles. He knew of some cops who liked a two-shot derringer while others carried sub-compacts. He figured the old cop would have a small revolver while the younger guy would carry a semi-auto. Working in security had brought him into contact with police, and sometimes, while he was getting information for a report, they would grab a coffee in the cafeteria of the building he was protecting and talk.

Vance tried to appear nonchalant, but he couldn't help fidgeting. Stepping back with his left foot, Vance scratched at his chin scruff, his other hand finding the crook of his elbow. The Thinker Posture, as some called it, effectively hid his fighting stance. Maybe these guys weren't cops. Could they be employed by the Tong? Anything was possible. The Asian cop looked him up and down, appraising him, before shifting his foot slightly to defend a kick to the balls. This guy had some combatives training, Vance thought.

"Detective Christian Keikan, Providence PD," the Asian detective said, flashing his badge. "Can we talk?"

At least these guys didn't work for Chinese mobsters. Hopefully. Cops he could handle, but they still made him nervous.

"Little out of your jurisdiction, Detective?" Vance asked. He'd seen this type of chiding done on TV and in the movies. Did he notice a little flash of anger behind the detectives' eyes? Vance knew he had to tread carefully. He didn't want to give the detective a reason to bring him in. Vance couldn't risk leaving Jade unprotected.

"I'm operating out of Newport," the detective said evenly. If he was angry or annoyed, his voice didn't betray his feelings. Coffee? I'm buying."

Keikan thumbed toward a diner next door.

"I'd rather not," Vance said. "Trying to enjoy what's left of a beautiful day."

"I know what you're doing. Don't worry, my partner will monitor the girl. I could arrest you for loitering. That would leave her unprotected."

This cop was pissing him off. Vance huffed in a breath, puffing it out of his nose, but nodded. What choice did he have? He didn't want to make a scene.

Vance entered the restaurant. Keikan tactically followed close behind.

The dining room remained bathed in shadow, as if the sun couldn't penetrate the windows.

They nestled into an even darker booth, away from the windows. Vance hated being separated from Jade. She was his responsibility.

"Let's see some ID," Keikan said.

"No problem," Vance said, feeling his brow break out in a sweat. "I've nothing to hide."

That wasn't exactly true. He wondered if his actions with the Kaiden had finally caught up to him. He hoped the perspiration didn't make him seem suspicious, or worse, guilty.

The detective took the driver's license and jotted down the information into a pocket spiral-bound notebook.

A fifty-something waitress asked if they were ready to order. She looked like she had been working by the sea her whole life.

"Two coffees," Keikan said, placing a twenty-dollar bill on the table. "We won't be long."

She gave a stilted smile, that brightened her worry lines and walked away.

"Now your cellphone," Keikan said. Vance hesitated. "Don't worry. I just want your number."

Vance slid the burner to him. Keikan took more notes.

"Who are you working for?" Keikan asked, sliding the phone back across the table.

"Nobody," Vance said.

"So, why are you here with Jade Maramoto?" Keikan asked. Vance tried not to look surprised. "I saw you get out of the limo with her."

That was a lie.

"I'm a friend of the family," Vance said. That wasn't a lie, but not quite the truth. Sho hadn't given him a paycheck, per se. Technically, he wasn't working for him.

"You're friends with a Japanese mobster?" Keikan asked.

"Sho's a businessman," Vance said.

The detective gave a forced laugh and shook his head.

"That's what he told you? A businessman?"

"That's exactly what he is," Vance said, feeling defensive.

"Well, it's not surprising. He's not going to tell you he's a crime lord. Now, is he?"

"Crime lord?" Vance asked, a little too loudly. The waitress returned with their coffees. He waited for her to walk away before continuing. "I've only seen him teach martial arts. He doesn't have the attention span to be a threat. He's deteriorating mentally."

"Don't believe everything you hear or see," the detective said, busying himself adding milk and sugar to his coffee. The spoon tinkled the sides of the cup as he swirled the potion together.

This detective was very good at his job. Good at getting under Vance's skin. He had to play this carefully. Yet isn't that what Sho had told him, the shinobi hid their actions in obfuscation and illusion?

"Why do you say that?" Vance asked.

"Look, you're hired muscle. I get it. I'm willing to overlook that you're body guarding without a license. In this state, that's a crime. Unless you have one you want to share with me."

Vance let the silence settle over them. He wasn't going to admit to anything and he certainly didn't have a license. He didn't even know he needed one.

"With Sho, you're traveling down a one-way road, but I can help you," Keikan said. "What I'm getting at is, I could really use a man on the inside."

"What are you asking?"

"Be my eyes and ears. Maybe open a gate and let me on the property."

"You're out of your mind," Vance said flabbergasted.

"Listen, if you won't do it because it's the right thing, think about yourself. You don't want to end up in prison," Keikan said, taking a last swig of coffee. "And if you don't care about yourself, do it for the girl. She deserves a better life than one of a mob princess. If you hand over Sho, we won't prosecute you or her. I'll guarantee it."

"I'll think about it," Vance said, realizing he hadn't even touched his coffee. He knew cops could lie to him, make promises they wouldn't keep. Although, he didn't get that feeling from this detective.

"Think about this," Keikan said, pulling out an evidence bag filled with blood speckled senban shurikan. Vance involuntarily twitched when the metal hit the table. The racket drew the attention of a few customers. "You're in way too deep. You've already made a mistake. Eventually, I'll connect all the dots and arrest you. If you work with me, I won't be in a hurry to make any conclusions."

The detective retrieved the stars and hid them away in a suit pocket.

"Don't think too long," Keikan said, "Your time is running out."

Chapter Twenty-Four

Keikan returned to the Crown Vic. Hayden had kept the engine running.

"She's still shopping," Hayden said, looking bored.

"Let's leave before she sees us," Keikan said, licking his lips. He could taste the salt in the air. "She'll make a cop car a mile away."

Hayden nodded and rolled deftly into traffic.

"Learn anything?" Hayden asked.

Keikan recounted the details of the meeting. Vance was one cool character that was for sure. He didn't break under questioning and remained in a heightened state of awareness, careful of everything he said.

"Going to get your girlfriend involved?" Hayden asked.

"Girlfriend?" Keikan asked, confused.

"What's her name…? Oh, yeah. Stacy," Hayden said.

"Forgot about her," Keikan said. She wouldn't blip on his radar until needed.

"She hasn't forgotten about you," Hayden said with a wink.

"Guess not," Keikan said.

"Gonna see her?" Hayden asked.

Keikan thought for a moment. Asking her on a date might keep her on board. But if things didn't work out….

"No," Keikan said. "Not a good idea."

"Hope she's available when you need her," Hayden said.

"You and me both," Keikan said. "You and me both."

Chapter Twenty-Five

Vance opened the door for Jade. She scooted inside the limo, a shopping bag in tow.

If Jade had noticed his absence, she didn't show it. Sunglasses hid her emotion.

Vance scanned the area for threats before getting in the other side. If he missed something, he wouldn't know.

Jade placed the bag on the floor and poured herself another drink. Ice tinkled in the glass.

"Get anything good?" Vance asked absently. His attempt at conversation sounded awkward and hollow, like an out of touch parent trying to connect with a disinterested teenager.

"You're really not that observant, are you?" Jade asked, shaking her head.

"I don't follow," Vance said, bracing himself to take the brunt of an inside joke.

"Gorflands is a ladies' underwear shop," the driver chimed in, his grin widening.

"Oh!" Vance said, his face flushing hot, and gave them a sheepish smile.

Chapter Twenty-Six

"I see you've taken excellent care of my daughter," Sho said, as Vance exited the limo.

"I did my best," Vance said, letting guilt choose his words.

"I'm going to look at my stuff, Daddy," Jade said, bounding out once again before the driver could hold the door open.

"Enjoy," Sho called after her as she headed for the mansion. Sho turned back to face Vance. "I have a surprise for you, Mr. Palladian."

Sho led Vance into the mansion and to a loft on the third floor. The apartment included a modern kitchen area, a small dining table, a cushy leather sofa, and a wall mounted flat screen TV. Two folding screens partitioned off a bedroom space with a big comfortable bed and a rolltop desk, giving the illusion of privacy.

"It's yours if you want it," Sho said, flashing a wide grin.

"I'm shocked," Vance said. "I thought you wanted me…."

"I wanted to harden you," Sho said. "I wanted you to concentrate on training instead of creature comforts. Now that your education is complete, there's no reason for such an austere life."

"I don't know what to say," Vance said, overwhelmed.

"This is the least I can do for my daughter's protector. I'll have one of the staff send for your things shortly."

Sho turned to leave, but then turned on his heels.

"Why don't you dine with us tonight. I want you to bond with Jade. In time, she'll grow to trust you."

"Sure, dinner sounds great," Vance said convincingly, but he felt conflicted. He didn't want to get too close to Jade, and he was already telling lies of omission to Sho.

"Very good," Sho said. "I'll leave you to freshen up."

Preparing for a shower, he emptied his pants pockets.

The phone!

He still had it! A burner. A landline was curiously absent from his room, but now he could make a call. Snatching the detective's card from his jeans he flipped it around, looked at the embossed printing. Then he remembered something almost forgotten.

Vance slipped out of the room and down the stairs.

At the cottage, he loaded toiletries, towels, and a change of clothing into a duffel bag—his alibi if caught or questioned upon returning.

Feeling paranoid—worried that someone had bugged the cottage—he slipped behind his once humble abode.

Glancing around, he dialed, hoping it wouldn't go to voicemail.

"Murphy."

"Murph! This is Vance, man. How you doing?"

"Vance?" Murphy said, sounding shocked. "I thought you were dead. Where you been?"

Vance gave him a quick rundown, then asked him a favor.

"Can do, buddy. I can even do better than that. I have contacts everywhere," Murphy said, a smile coloring his voice. "It's rare that your best friend returns from the grave."

"I really appreciate it," Vance said. "How bout I call you in a few days?" Vance asked. "Then maybe we can meet up?"

"You bet your ass we can."

Chapter Twenty-Seven

"I just talked to a dead man," Keikan said looking over to Hayden. Hayden looked up from whatever he was doing at his desk, probably playing solitaire, or taking notes for his ghostwriter on a new book project.

Keikan was amazed this dinosaur could use a computer. He'd caught Hayden turning off the CPU by pressing the button on the ancient tower instead of going through the shutdown procedure. One day, Hayden would destroy the hard drive.

"Like a zombie?" Hayden said deadpan. He didn't sound like he was joking.

"They declared Vance Palladian dead," Keikan said.

"What happened?" Hayden asked.

That was a good question, and one not easily answered. The news stories were scant and vague. The police had taken a report, but the investigation went nowhere.

"He stopped a robbery at a convenience store. Protected a customer. Got brained by a bat for his troubles. Slipped into a coma and never awoke. There was an assumption that the plug was pulled. Declared dead over a year ago."

"I didn't know Sho was creating an undead army," Hayden said, straight faced again. "Who was the customer that got attacked?"

"That's the best part," Keikan said, "Jade Maramoto."

"Really? Hayden asked, shaking his head. "He saves Sho's daughter, and now he's employed as her bodyguard?"

"Crazier things have happened," Keikan said, nodding. Remembering.

"What's his past look like?"

"Used to run a martial arts school in Providence. Taught kwan-style Tae Kwon Do, like the Tang Soo Do variant," Keikan said, but changed tracks when he noticed Hayden's blank expression.

"He won his share of full-contact tournaments. That was back before MMA became all the rage. Moonlighted in private security to pay the bills. Recently widowed before the coma. He's the only child of deceased parents and a stepmother. Grew up in Wellington, Massachusetts, and doesn't have a criminal record."

"So, where does this leave us?"

"I think Palladian is our key inside Maramoto's estate."

"So, we need to go talk to him again," Hayden said, his expression sour. No doubt he was dreading more stakeouts.

"I have a better idea."

Chapter Twenty-Eight

Andre Murphy sat in his Subaru Outback, a ubiquitous family wagon that blended into most neighborhoods. He wore a charcoal gray button-down shirt, no tie, and rubber soled casual loafers that looked dressy enough, were comfortable, and allowed him to run, hop a fence, or defend himself. He clipped a tactical pen made of unbreakable aircraft aluminum to the pocket of his chinos. He also carried an easily concealable .32 caliber pistol. The small rounds weren't man-stoppers but were better than nothing.

Crusader Security & Investigations had him staking out Barry Saunders. Saunders had filed worker's comp claims regarding an alleged back injury.

He lived with his wife and three children in a Cape style home, sans chimney, like the rest of the street, built right after World War II for returning soldiers.

Sander's former employer wanted photographic or video evidence of the complainant lifting heavy items, working under the table, or hell, even doing back flips. So far—no dice. This guy might be legit. If not, at least he was smart enough to lie low.

Real private investigation was nothing like the movies. Murphy worked the stakeout alone. He liked that just fine, performing surveillance, an activity most found boring.

He couldn't pass the time reading or scrolling through social media. Focus and situational awareness were crucial.

Instead, like today, he streamed audiobooks in the background. He mainly listened to spy thrillers, and action & adventure novels, and more personal development programs than he'd care to admit.

Surveillance put a strain not only on the investigator's focus, but also their bladder. A tightly sealed Gatorade bottle sat at the ready for bathroom breaks. Purel antibacterial hand wipes kept his hygiene at an acceptable level.

"Oh shit!" Murphy said under his breath. A large man stormed out of the house, heading straight for the Subaru wagon. Saunders was on to him.

Trying to look nonchalant and pretending he hadn't seen the angry man; he removed his keys from the ignition and silenced the audiobook.

Murphy inhaled deeply, grabbed his clipboard filled with dummy catalogs, and nonchalantly exited his vehicle.

The agency had helped him create a detailed backstory. As far as anyone knew, he worked as a salesperson. A stack of business cards with an embossed phone number that would be answered by a secretary who would confirm he worked for the fake company.

He wasn't even supposed to tell his own mother that he did investigations. All it would take was a slipup to get him killed.

"Who the fuck are you?" Saunders asked, his face flushing a light red.

"Excuse me?" Murphy asked, moving to the front of the car while filming the confrontation from the clipboard's hidden camera.

"You hard of hearing, buddy?" Saunders said, closing the distance. "You been sitting here all damn day spying on me."

"Listen, man," Murphy said. "Don't get paranoid. I'm just a salesman trying to make a buck."

Murphy could have easily pressed the tactical pen into service as a shank or kubaton or reached into his pocket full of fun and brandished the firearm. The small rounds in the .32 were by no means manstoppers, but they would do damage, even kill if they hit a vital spot. He hadn't reached that level of escalation. With luck, he could defuse the situation.

"What you call me?" the man said, throwing a wide, looping sucker punch.

Murphy slipped the attack using the principles of AikiJujutsu, moving inside Sander's reach, controlling the space. Pushing when pulled, and in this case, pulling when pushed. Then performing a street-modified judo *O-goshi*, hip throw.

Saunders broke his fall with outstretched hands, scrambled back up. Did this guy really need workers comp? Murphy had gone easy on him. More force and Barry would have eaten concrete.

"You son of a bitch!" Saunders screamed, throwing a right cross.

Murphy shifted his weight, allowing the punch to sail past his right ear. That one had starch on it. If it had connected….

Murphy turned, captured Sander's momentum along with his arm, tossing him with a *seo nage*, shoulder throw.

Sanders landed on his back with a satisfying thud. He lay on the ground, the wind knocked out of him.

"You're lucky I'm not calling the police," Murphy said, rushing back to the wagon. "The things I do to sell this shit."

Chapter Twenty-Nine

Crusader Security & Investigations stood off Route 9 in Westborough, Massachusetts, a two-story whitewashed structure that housed human resources on the first floor and operations, investigations, and training on the second.

Murphy began his career as a process server for law firms and courthouses but was required by law to be under the employ of a detective agency before going out on his own. He had worked at Crusader long enough to apply for his own detective license and hang a shingle, but he couldn't get himself to pull the trigger on his own business.

Now he might not have a choice.

He was in for it.

Classical music tickled his ears as he entered the building. The neat reception area presented a corporate air, a white-collar oasis in a blue-collar industry.

He approached the receptionist.

Lissy Guerra straddled her rough upbringing with the demands of presenting a genteel public image. She usually fell on the side of failing.

How long would she last? She'd already kept the job for over a year. He thought it a minor miracle.

He liked her, but only in a platonic way. She already had a boyfriend, anyway. One who was always getting her in trouble.

She raised a finger to acknowledge him while finishing the call.

"So, what are you doing here, Murphy?" Lissy said, putting the receiver on the cradle. She scribbled on a sticky note and then gave him a wry smile. "It's not payday."

"Yeah, I try to stay out of here. I get in trouble when I'm in the office too long."

"I hear you," Lissy said. "Wish I had that luxury. I'm always getting into something."

"One day I'll go out on my own and take you away from all this."

"Yeah? Just like Charlie's Angels, huh?" she said, turning to profile in her swivel chair, raising her arms as she clasped her hands into the shape of a gun, recreating the iconic image, then laughed.

"Exactly like that," Murphy said, rolling his eyes. "You know if Donovan is busy?"

She dialed Donavan's executive assistant.

"Yeah, Murphy's here. Wants to see Rob. Yeah, yeah, here comes trouble. Okay." She looked up at him. "He's free. Go right up."

"I *will* take you away from this," Murphy said, climbing the stairs to the second floor.

"Yeah. Sure, sure. Talk to you later, Murph."

Rob Donovan sat behind a gargantuan desk strewn with paper, a pair of reading glasses perched on the tip of his nose. He pecked at a computer, years out of date.

"Take a seat," Donovan said as he continued hunting and pecking. "Give me a sec."

Murphy plopped into the faux leather chair in front of the desk. Donovan had found perhaps the lowest chair available to accentuate his seat of power.

Murphy looked at Donovan's mementos from the police force. He had never asked Donovan why he'd left law enforcement. Figured it was none of his business.

Anything could have happened, and he guessed it might have been something terrible.

"What's up?" Donovan asked when he finished typing. He placed his palms on the desk as if to say, you have my undivided attention. Donovan had that haunted five-hundred-yard stare in his eyes that never dissipated, even when he smiled.

"Good news, bad news," Murphy said, trying to sound confident. "I got video of Saunders taking a swing at someone."

"Who did he swing at?" Donovan asked, his intonation deepening, the air rushing out with the words. He already knew the answer.

Murphy splayed his hands.

"Hand it over," Donovan said.

Murphy retrieved the flash drive. Donovan snatched it from Murphy's fingers. After fiddling with it, he finally seated the drive into the port.

Donovan watched the video silently, his expression unreadable. When he finished, he turned back to Murphy.

"You should have stayed in the car."

"I know."

"This is an S.I.R." Donovan said. Murphy nodded. A Serious Incident Report. The report needed to be filed and sent to corporate immediately. Murphy's punishment wouldn't rest with Donovan, but with the top brass.

"I'm going to forget I ever saw this," Donovan said. "This the only copy?"

"Yeah," Murphy said.

"And you didn't leave any literature behind with the dummy company name on it?"

"No."

Donovan turned to his computer and right clicked on the icon.

"Deleted."

"Rob! What are you doing? We could have nailed that guy!"

"You know that video would mean your job and litigation for Crusader. The client might win the case, but we'd all get sued for whatever damages the court awarded."

"So that's it. We're back to square one."

"You're not back to anything. I'm taking you off the case."

"You're joking."

"I don't joke about these things. You know how hard it is to continue a surveillance once an investigator has been made. You're going to take unpaid leave, so I don't have to put you on official suspension. You'll cool off and reflect on your actions.

"You're one of our best investigators, Murph. I can't afford to lose you. We all fuck up from time to time. This was your time. I'll cover for you once, never again. Just remember that when you have an urge to play cowboy."

"Okay, great. I don't like it."

"You don't have to like it," Donovan opened a drawer in his desk and pulled out a lock box. He retrieved a wad of bills and counted out $500.00. "Petty cash. I know you don't make enough to take unpaid leave. Use this to eat out for a couple of weeks. Save the receipts."

"Thanks Rob," Murphy said, grabbed the bills, and stuffed them into his jeans.

"Do me a solid?" Murphy asked. This was as good a time as any. Better get to Rob while he's feeling generous.

"Seriously? I just did you a favor. Two actually."

"Yeah, I know. And I owe you. You mind?" Murphy asked, pointing to a pad and pen on the desk.

"Go ahead."

"Check on a couple guys for me?" Murphy said, scribbling the names on the pad. "I wouldn't ask, but I have a friend who's in some serious shit. I know you have better connections in Rhode Island than I do."

Donovan looked at the paper and nodded, blowing air from his nose. "I'll make some calls and let you know later tonight. When you're back on salary, you owe me a beer and some shots. Lots of shots."

"You got it, boss," Murphy said, making for the door. "I won't let you down again."

"You're damn right you won't," Donovan called after him. "You won't be working here if you do."

Murphy returned to the one bedroom second-floor apartment he liked to think of as his bachelor pad. Although he kept the place clean, he'd never take a lady there to entertain.

Rents remained cheaper in poorer neighborhoods, and on his salary, he needed cheap, and he especially needed his ex-wife to think he needed cheap.

He didn't mind paying to feed and clothe little Malcolm and Imani, but he wasn't' keen on buying new outfits and vacations for her and her boyfriend.

He'd been smart all those years, if not a little cynical, squirreling away money in his brother's name. Jalen was always savvy with stocks, helping his big bro build a substantial nest egg, one that he wouldn't touch until the time was right. If the ex-wife ever found out about that money, she'd want half. When the time was right, his brother would "invest" that money in Murphy's detective agency, and he would be in business.

Murphy placed a takeout bag on the kitchen counter.

He dumped his messenger bag on the couch, stowed his leather jacket in the closet, and tuned the tv to 24-hour cable news. White noise.

He placed the tactical knife and pen into the top drawer of his bedroom nightstand and returned his gun to the safe in the bottom drawer.

A battle-ready katana made by an American sword maker (Japanese swords were hard to come by and expensive, remaining illegal to export from Japan) who remained true to the old Japanese ways, stood at the ready on a vertical stand by the bed.

If he couldn't get to the gun, the katana was his safeguard. The literature said the sword was sharp enough to cut a person in half. Murphy hoped he'd never find out if the claims were accurate or mere hyperbole. He'd never get the blood out of the carpet.

Ready to relax while researching, he plated food, grabbed a craft beer, and settled into the computer nook beside the couch.

He began with a Google search, copying pertinent information, links, and notes into a Word document. Lots of useful information.

Plenty of newspaper articles had been archived along with images. A satellite photo of the Maramoto estate. Navigable street level photos.

He performed virtual recon like this before any insurance stakeout, but he knew the map was not the terrain. Everything looked different at the location.

Then he searched for info Vance requested. He pulled up detailed histories and social media discussions. Two bottles of beer drained while hunting and pecking, clicking and scrolling.

Some of it just confirmed what Murphy already suspected.

His phone rang. He looked at the number.

"What's up, boss?"

Donovan filled him in. Murphy typed furiously, filling in the gaps. He made a few minutes of small talk with Donovan and then hung up.

Vance had gotten himself into some serious shit.

Murphy decided he'd wait a couple days, try to be patient. After that, he'd have to go down to Newport and find him.

Chapter Thirty

Vance showered and changed into a button-down blue shirt, khaki pants, and a pair of slip-on dress loafers.

He considered dabbing on a hint of Dolce and Gabbana but thought better of it. He didn't want Sho thinking anything untoward of him, and besides, this was supposed to be a bonding dinner—not a date with his daughter.

When Vance arrived, Sho waited at the head of the table. Vance took a seat across from an empty chair. A place had been set, but where was Jade?

"How do you like your room?" Sho asked before taking a sip of wine.

"It's very nice. I appreciate it," Vance said, uncomfortable with the hospitality. Especially now that his trust of Sho was waning. Confrontation would eventually have to be put on the agenda, but now wasn't the time.

Jade entered, shades on.

Sho stood. Vance followed suit. The chivalric ritual of standing when a woman entered a room appealed to him. It spoke to the splendor of a bygone age.

"Why is he here?" Jade asked. Evidently, she had also brought her attitude.

"Take off your glasses," Sho said.

Jade obeyed, scowling at Vance. Yet, a hint of playfulness seeped through.

"When you have to trust one another," Sho continued, "it's good to break bread."

"May I have a glass of wine?" Jade asked, turning to her father.

"You may have two if you don't spend the entire night in a foul mood."

"I can't promise anything," Jade said.

"What was that?"

"Yes, Daddy."

"Good. The server will arrive shortly," Sho said rising.

"Where are you going, Daddy?" Jade asked.

"I'm having a sandwich sent up to my room. You have no need for a chaperone."

With that, Sho strode out, leaving Jade and Vance to their own company.

Vance shifted in his seat.

The server entered with a bottle of wine.

"Whisky," Jade said.

The woman abruptly turned, set the bottle on a side table, and exited the room.

She returned with two fluted Glencairn glasses and an ornate decanter.

The server poured a dram and set the glass to Jade's right.

Vance waved the server away as she approached.

"You're not on duty," Jade said. "Have a drink."

Vance nodded. If he was going to ape the rich, he might as well try something expensive. He'd had nothing but bottom shelf "call whiskey" on the rocks or in cola.

The server poured his dram and then left the dining room.

"Sure, you don't want wine?" Jade asked. "Single malt scotch is an acquired taste."

"What makes you think I haven't tried scotch before?" Vance asked, trying to sound confident.

Jade smirked.

"You're in luck," she said. "This is a Speyside. Twelve-years old. Light and fruity. Whisky with training wheels. Sip it like wine."

Vance nodded, picking up his glass to shoot it down the ol' hatch. A smooth burn down his throat. He tried to shake the feeling away.

"If you're thirsty, drink water."

Vance set the glass on the table. Jade poured him another.

"I'll show you how to do it. First, aerate the scotch," Jade said as she swirled the pale liquid in the glass. Vance followed her lead. "Now nose the whisky gently."

He took a sniff.

"What did you smell?" Jade asked.

"Alcohol," Vance said, and smiled.

"Not very sophisticated, are we?" Jade said. "Over time, you'll pick up hints of vanilla, plum, and oak, among others. Now sip it. Hold it in your mouth for a moment before you swallow."

Vance took a taste. Taking his time, it was easy to notice that this whisky was the smoothest he had ever had but found that the vanilla overpowered the other flavors. The finish heated his mouth rather than burning his esophagus. A pleasing sensation.

She looked on expectantly.

"I like it," he said. "But it's a little sweet for my tastes."

"You'll have to try a dram of an Islay," Jade said, pronouncing it *Eye-La*. "Probably more your style."

"What's that taste like?"

"Smoke, cough sweets," Jade said. "Old, tanned leather."

Vance laughed. Jade laughed despite herself. Yeah, he probably would like that. She already knew him too well.

"So, is Jade the English version of your Japanese name?" Vance said, easing into the conversation. He had questions but wanted to be careful how he posed them. If the whisky gave him the nerve, maybe it would relax some of her defensiveness and inhibitions, allowing her to confide in him.

"My Japanese name is *Gyokko*." she said. "It means Jade Tiger.

"The green in my contact lenses is the closest I could get to the color."

"I never noticed," Vance said. "They didn't stand out at all."

Jade laughed again. If you spent enough time with a glass of whisky, the ice would eventually melt.

"Gyokko Maramoto. It rhymes," Vance mused, smiling. Jade smiled back.

The server brought in the first course: soup and salad, and they settled down to eat.

Sho really knows how to supper. He could really get used to this.

Why did he want to mess this whole thing up? Was he crazy?

"Did your father name you?" Vance asked. An innocent question. Yet, a darkness flittered behind her eyes. Her expression didn't change.

"No," she said mechanically. "It was my mother's choice. She passed, if you're wondering."

"I'm sorry," Vance said. He couldn't get himself to ask how it had happened. The death of parents wasn't usual. Sho was already in his seventies. Even though women often lived longer, it wasn't unheard of for the wife to die first. "Both my parents died when I was much younger. Not to mention a stepmother."

"We are both incomplete," Jade said.

"Yes, we are," Vance said, flashing a wan smile.

The loss of a parent at a young age was said to stunt the psyche. There were psychologists who believed you could never get over something like that, and the trauma would be in effect for the rest of that person's life. Vance didn't like to think they were both so wounded they would never recover. He was sure that so much death had unconsciously affected his life choices, but was the wound so great it would never heal, was something that could never be overcome? He hoped not.

They finished their salads, making small talk until the server brought in the main course: filet minion with sweet potato on the side. Vance took a bite—perfectly cooked, tender, and succulent. He wanted to forget his old life, and the detective who'd cemented his suspicions. But he could already feel the old paladin within reawakening.

"I feel your dad isn't being upfront with me."

"Is that a question?" Jade asked, taking a bite of her steak, leaning forward, giving him a sly grin.

"Only if you want to answer," Vance said.

"Maybe he's not the only one," Jade said, flashing a smile of her own before returning to her dinner.

After dinner, Jade excused herself, and Vance returned to his room. The ice had melted a little, but there was too much to defrost for one evening. Either that, or she was playing hard to get. He'd have liked to think the latter.

He couldn't deny he was drawn to her. Shit. He was too young for a midlife crisis. His attraction to her wasn't good for either of them.

From his underwear drawer he retrieved the cell phone and slipped outside into the darkness. Stepping away from the mansion he hoped to be far from prying eyes and ears. For all he knew, Sho had bugged every shrub, every sapling. Perhaps every blade of grass.

"Got any information for me, buddy?" Vance asked when Murphy answered. He felt hopeful. Murphy had access to a phone and a computer. He could certainly get more information than Vance ever could sequestered inside the estate.

"Plenty," Murphy said. Vance's hope rose. "Meet me tomorrow night. I'll give you the scoop in person."

Could he leave the estate without arousing suspicion?

Sho hadn't implied he was a prisoner. He had access to a car, a credit card, and money. He could transform and fly out but thought showing up as tengu might be a little awkward.

Jade seemed more content. Vance couldn't see her sneaking off into the night again. At least he didn't think she would for a while.

"I'm in," Vance said, taking down the address.

"One more thing," Murphy said. "Just be careful. You're in deeper than you think."

Chapter Thirty-One

The next morning, Vance awoke to the luxury of the mansion. For a moment he thought he was still in the cottage.

He needed to stay occupied until the evening. Vance looked out the window. He could see the Teahouse Dojo in the distance. He opened a window and put his face near the screen. The sun had already warmed the air. With a flash of inspiration, he slipped on swim trunks under his track pants.

Outside, he greeted an Indian summer. A dying harvest god's last gasp, before a wintery grave. The idyllic day eased Vance's turbulent soul.

Jogging across the estate, glad for the running shoes (tabbi offered no structural support), his button-down shirt ruffled in the breeze.

At the bluff, he followed the narrow path until he came upon an unlikely valley where twin waterfalls raged on either side of the embankment.

The torrent raced over slimy rocks and traced rivulets that led down to the ocean. The water fed from streams that ran through woods where he had killed the deer, and perhaps originated underground.

Fresh air rose with the spray, relaxing him.

Warm from the run, Vance fired off punch kick combinations. Blending the movements seamlessly. Enjoying the physicality.

He missed spontaneous exercise and for the first time in a long time felt comfortable in his own skin again.

Once he had worked up a sweat, he stripped down to his trunks and left his clothing far from the stream.

Muscles rippling, undulating under his skin, the transformation complete: from an invalid to a healthy specimen—his body a weapon. Not only had he been rehabilitated, but they had also remade him better than before. The night's metamorphosis forgotten; he could live fully in daylight.

Sho and Kevin had forged his body and mind like the metal of the earth, represented by the sword he had wielded, tempered him in the fire he had walked, and scattered his past and his old identity to the wind, as he was perilously hung off a cliff by only his ankles with Kevin's grip his only tether.

Now he needed purification, a baptism of sorts to purge him of the darkness and return him to the man he was before the coma.

Vance passed barefoot over warm stones past the waterfall to his left and toward a similar waterfall to his right. Lowering himself into the shallow pool of refreshing water, he navigated a floor of polished stone and then slipped behind the waterfall's torrent.

Behind him, the cave lay in total darkness, the splash of water echoing deep inside the cavern.

Stepping forward, he entered the deluge, allowed the frigid water to blast him. The cold loosened a howl deep from within. His scream echoed into the cavern behind him. Backing away he slipped, then regained his footing. Emerging from behind the waterfall back into the light, he wiped away water to clear his vision. The water in the pool now felt tepid on his skin having experienced the extreme cold of the moving water.

Jade had magically appeared at the waterfall diagonally across from his. Her black string bikini left very little to the imagination. Her shapely curves as enticing and heady as the booze, wealth, and power the Kaiden had offered. He climbed out of the pool; the shock of the cold water kept him from embarrassing himself.

Hugging his body against the chill, the sun slowly warmed him.

Their gazes met. She gave him a wink and a slight smile.

Assuming the lotus position on a dry rock, Jade closed her eyes. She weaved fingers through *mudra* kuji-in hand signs. Her arms rose, fell, and then pushed out, before moving onto the next. *Mantra,* words of power, echoed off stones, drifted over the roaring waterfall.

After cycling through four sets, she opened her eyes, a serenity twinkling behind them, and submerged and slipped behind the waterfall, into the torrent, as Vance himself had done.

The water soaked her skin and tore at her suit. Even in the chaos of the cascade, she remained relaxed. Returning to the lotus position, she cycled through the mudra again.

Vance followed her example. Entering the waterfall, he allowed the numbing cold to recede into the background, as his breathing and concentration took prominence.

The procedure he knew. Kevin had taught it to him. These were the nine levels of power that derived from Mikkyo Buddhism. They were said to give the practitioner preternatural abilities. The ninja was said to have used them, but also the samurai. He wondered what it would do for a tengu.

He intertwined his fingers and worked through each procedure to set his mind for each attribute and ability.

Rin, the Tibetan Thunderbolt, offered the strength of mind, body and an unmovable spirit.

Pyo, the Great Diamond, increased energy within the body.

Toh, the Outer Lion, increased one's will and courage.

Shah, the Inner Lion, helped the practitioner to heal themselves and others.

Kai, the Outer bonds Fist, gave the power of precognition.

Jin, the Inner Bonds Fist, bestowed the power of telepathy.

Retsu, the Wisdom Fist, fine-tuned the practitioner's awareness of the universe.

Zai, the Ring of the Sun, allowed the practitioner to control all the elements in nature.

Zen, the Concealed Fist, gave the enlightenment attained by the Buddha.

Once the exercise was completed, Vance stood despite the force of the water trying to keep him down.

Sopping wet, yet exhilarated, Vance emerged from the waterfall victorious.

He smiled, looked to the waterfall where Jade had been just moments before.

She had vanished.

Chapter Thirty-Two

That night, Vance slipped from the mansion into the darkness. He hurried to the carport, his heart racing, nerves prickling. He was taking a big chance leaving the estate without telling anyone. Now that he was doing it, the whole thing didn't seem like such a good idea.

In the carport, squatting, he ran his fingers under the Corvette until he felt the raised plastic tracker. He let it clatter to the concrete, as if it had come loose on its own.

The Corvette roared to life, and he made his way to the gate with the headlights off.

Once he reached the guard shack, he applied the break and waited.

The guard squinted to see who sat in the darkened interior of the vehicle. Vance snapped on the inside light. Holding his breath, he waved at the guard.

Would the guard let him out? What would he do if he didn't?

Nodding, the guard raised the gate.

Exhaling, Vance relaxed his grip on the steering wheel. Heart rate lowering, Vance merged into traffic and put peddle to metal.

An hour later he turned off the Massachusetts Turnpike, known colloquially as *The Pike* by Bostonians, and navigated the streets of Brighton.

Where Providence felt somewhat generic to Vance, Brighton had a definite Boston vibe. Brownstones and mom & pop business rolled by. Stop and go traffic the whole way.

A cramped public lot hidden behind a graffiti covered brick building provided parking. A heavily congested liquor store to his left cast the adjoining parking lot in garish phosphorescent light. He eased into the last spot, thankful for his good fortune. Boston parking was a bitch. He only hoped some asshole didn't scratch or ding the vehicle.

Jaunting through an alleyway, he emerged onto a heavily congested sidewalk filled with college students, beatniks, and hoody wearing denizens. Half a block and he reached his destination.

A block up, Vance found the building. He climbed a set of concrete steps to a fingerprint smeared glass door. A large gold 126 stenciled on the framed window above. Vance tried the door. Locked. He pressed the intercom button labeled Suite 9. Then a buzz and a click and he was inside, ascending the grimy staircase.

A young man, no older than mid-twenties, wearing a black hakima over a crisp white dogi uniform, greeted him.

"Can I help you?" the young man asked, a tinge of suspicion coloring his voice.

"Vance Palladian," Vance said, extending his hand. "Master Murphy is expecting me."

"Paul Davidson," the young man said, giving Vance a firm handshake. "I'll bring you right in.

"We get troublemakers and challengers sometimes. It's my job to make sure you had good intentions."

"What would happen if I didn't have good intentions?" Vance asked.

Paul Davidson thought for a moment.

"I'd have to knock you out, of course," the young man said, then smiled. Then they both laughed good naturedly.

"Of course," Vance said with a laugh.

The young man's response didn't surprise him. Not one bit. Back in the day, Gold's reputation kept away challengers. Word traveled fast though the small town of Wellington, but Metro-Aiki resided in the heart of the city where a reputation could take longer to establish, and with the increased capacity in population, and dozens of martial arts schools, came more potential challengers.

In modern times, this had become a business tactic. If the challenger could beat and humiliate the head instructor, the challenger's school might see increased enrollment as word spread. The defeat could drive the instructor out of business.

Vance wouldn't put up with that type of nonsense. He had nothing to prove. He'd ask the challenger to leave, and if they didn't leave, he'd just call the police.

If he had to subdue him in the meantime, he had no problem with that. Some of his black belt students, not yet secure with themselves, longed to prove themselves in that type of a duel, but he'd always admonished them feeling that type of behavior an affront to all he taught.

Whatever happened to that guy?

It didn't matter anyway, that sort of thing went out more than a decade ago. Some habits were hard to break.

At the end of the hall, they reached a door with Metro-Aiki stenciled on a glass window.

Vance followed Paul's lead, pulling off his sneakers and stowing them in a shoe cubby just outside the door. The young man quietly turned the handle and bowed before entering.

Framed in cedar wood, the dojo was decorated with scrolls painted with Japanese calligraphy, weapons racks, and at the kamiza (seat of honor), a kamidana miniature wood house sat on a shelf high on the wall. These accruements gave the air of entering a training hall in Asia instead of a converted office space on the East Coast.

Despite the violent origins of the war arts, the dojo felt tranquil. Perhaps, created by a Japanese version of *feng shui* Vance didn't have an eye for.

Murphy stood, sword raised, in the center of the dojo. He wore a kimono top with Hakama.

Three swordsmen wearing the same attire fanned out around him.

Vance smiled. He was looking forward to watching Murphy thrash someone besides himself. Padding over cool gray matting, he settled in next to Paul and another dozen students sitting in *seiza* by the nearest wall.

Murphy, graceful as ever, shifted his feet, aligning himself for the killing blow. His hakima trousers gave off the illusion of floating across the floor.

The circle of katana armed opponents rotated around him clockwise while he moved widdershins.

In a flash of movement, they were upon him. Murphy parried and struck, symbolically cutting down all his opponents before wiping his blade and returning it to the scabbard.

The students applauded. Vance clapped as well. He had to hand it to Murphy; age hadn't slowed him down. Not one bit.

"Hold your applause," Murphy said with a wink. "Just throw money. I think we'll end here tonight."

Then a twinkle of recognition in his eyes.

"Look who we've got here, class," Murphy said, grinning widely. "A genuine paladin. Isn't that right, Vance?"

Murphy said it like: gen-you-wine Pal-a-dine.

"That's what they called me," Vance said, playing along.

"Well, Mr. Paladin, would you like to pick up a weapon and fight for the cause?" Murphy asked, speaking normally now.

"Don't mind if I do," Vance said, preparing for another ass whooping. But he had a few new tricks up his sleeve. He hoped Murphy wouldn't catch on until it was too late.

"Mind if I take that one?" Vance asked, pointing to the far wall.

"The *odachi*?" Murphy asked.

"I need all the advantage I can get," Vance said, admiring the long sword. A predecessor to the katana, the odachi was mainly used to fight in fields or on horseback.

"Over-compensating," Murphy asked, and then chuckled. The rest of the class laughed good-naturedly along with him. "Go on. Let's see what you got."

Vance hefted the sword. To pull this off, he'd have to hide his intentions and sell Murphy on the illusion.

Murphy snatched a *yari* spear from a weapons rack.

"Ain't no way Paladin gonna get the longest weapon in this joint," Murphy said.

The students laughed again.

Vance and Murphy bowed to each other and then assumed fighting stances.

Vance held the sword awkwardly, left hand forward.

Murphy looked at him suspiciously.

Vance shrugged.

This was a gamble.

The room fell quiet and Vance focused solely on Murphy. He could do that here. These students lived honorably, by the code of the samurai. There would be no tricks.

The tension grew between them. Both men waited for the right moment to attack.

Vance held his sword in *Chuden no kamae* (middle posture), pointing the sword tip toward Murphy's left eye, creating an illusion of an opening, baiting Murphy to strike.

Murphy took the bait, cutting downward with the spear, bending forward to amplify his motion.

Vance blocked the spear's downward motion with the flat of his blade. Stepping diagonally to the outside, he cut down. With immaculate control, he placed the blade on the back of Murphy's neck. The students gasped.

Vance withdrew his sword.

A moment of uncomfortable silence.

"You know, Paladin," Murphy said, finally. "You're making me look bad in front of my students."

Everyone laughed, and the tension dissipated.

"Turnabout's fair play," Vance said. "Your Sensei did the same in front of my students."

More laughter.

"Vance Palladian earned his black belt with me way back when. And I taught him everything he knows," Murphy said, putting an arm around Vance's shoulder. "He's a tricky little devil. Time for you to be the teacher. Tell them how you beat me."

Devil? More like a demon, Vance thought.

"I used shinobi techniques," Vance said. All the students looked interested, but he could still feel Murphy's cynicism despite his display of skill. He explained what Sho had taught him. "It was more strategy than skill," Vance said before giving them a basic rundown. "I never thought I'd get the chance to try it out."

"I'm glad I gave you the opportunity," Murphy said rolling his eyes. "Look, you wait here and don't be disappearing on me in a puff of smoke or anything. I need to bow these people out."

Vance nodded and stood back while everyone took their places. Murphy and his black belts knelt in seiza at the head of the class. The students lined up according to rank, across from them.

The black belts turned and faced the *kamidalla*, a wooden house that represented the spiritual seat of the dojo, held their hands in front of their foreheads, like in prayer to some ancient deity. Much of the ceremony had been lifted from Shinto, an indigenous religion and the oldest in Japan.

"*Shiken haramitsu daikomyo*, lead us to enlightenment with a merciful, sincere, attuned and dedicated heart," Murphy said.

The class performed a seated bow, clapped their hands in unison once, bowed again, and then clapped twice, releasing the prayer to the heavens.

The black belts turned to face the students.

"*Sensei ne-ray*, bow to the teacher," Paul Davidson said. His prominence in the ritual signaled him out as the senior student.

The students bowed.

"*Domo arigato gozaimashita*, thank you very much for training," they all said in unison.

Then Murphy bowed to the students repeating the sentiment.

"All right," Murphy said. "We're finished for tonight. Make sure you write down as much as you can remember in your notebooks. Especially that shinobi stuff. You might never see it again."

When all the students had filed out, Murphy brought Vance to his cramped office.

The chief instructors' certificates adorned the walls, ranking from every A-Z organization.

The uninitiated might find it impressive, but Vance knew that these associations were a dime a dozen. In an industry that wasn't regulated, you had to take any type of certification with a wary eye. Not that he thought martial arts schools should be regulated. There was too much politics and infighting in the martial arts for that.

The only thing that impressed Vance was skill. The teacher either had it or not. He assumed the head teacher must have had the goods or Murphy wouldn't have bothered with the place. Murphy knew quality when he saw it. He had Gold as a reference point. That was good enough for Vance.

Murphy grabbed his duffle bag, dropped it on the desk, and pulled out fresh clothing and a towel.

"I have a lot to go over," Murphy said as he stripped down and toweled off. "You hungry?"

"I could eat," Vance said.

"Yeah, me too. And I'm thirsty for a beer," Murphy said. "I did all the leg work. You're buying."

Vance followed Murphy's Outback until they reached a strip mall on Beacon Street in Newton.

Vance pulled the Corvette into a cramped parking space in front of the South Pacific Chinese Restaurant, scratches, and dings still on his mind.

"Nice car," Murphy said, and whistled.

"It's not mine," Vance said, nodding his head. Then he pointed his thumb at the restaurant, looking as if he was going to bum a ride.

"I thought this place closed."

"Maybe they didn't get the memo," Murphy said with a wink.

They entered the restaurant. Vance hadn't been to this place in forever, but the decor always transported him back twenty years. The place was like walking into a time warp. The nostalgia comforted him.

The hostess, a young Chinese woman, brought them into a back room framed by palm wood, lined with booths on the right and longer tables on the left.

Mosaics and murals of South Pacific island-life adorned the walls. A dark knotted wood steepled ceiling gave the illusion of a Hawaiian hut.

They passed a family of six where a smartly dressed matriarch ordered Shirley Temples with extra cherries for her three grandchildren.

"How do I have grandchildren, Steve?" she asked the waiter. "I'm not a day older than sweet sixteen."

Vance smiled despite himself. It was like walking into someone else's happy memory.

The hostess placed two menus at a booth across from the family.

As soon as they slid in, an older Chinese waiter approached them.

"Murphy, good to see you," the waiter said.

"Steve, buddy. Meet my friend, Vance," Murphy said. "Made black belt together."

"Is that so?" Steve asked, raising an eyebrow.

"Well, we're just American black belts," Vance said. Steve laughed warmly.

"Steve is a Gung Fu man," Murphy said.

"Non-traditional Wing Chun," Steve said. "I also train in Filipino Arts."

"You teach?" Vance asked.

"Steve and the owner, John, put their kids through college working here," Murphy said.

"You can't earn a living teaching martial arts," Steve said. "Especially teaching the old ways."

"Tell me about it," Vance said.

"Now, let me get you two a drink."

"Bourbon on the rocks," Murphy said.

"I thought you wanted a beer?" Vance asked.

"I did, but you're buying, so bourbon it is. Top shelf. Have the bartender surprise me."

Vance ordered a beer, and Steve went to get the drinks.

The nook created by the booth, and the murmur of the patrons, gave at least the illusion of privacy. Enough privacy, or enough of an illusion, that Vance felt comfortable speaking freely.

They waited until Steve returned with the drinks and took their order before getting down to business.

"Lay it on me," Vance said once he had a sip of his drink. The bitter IPA lingered on his tongue. "Everything."

"Okay. First, nice trick with the sword, but it's not ninjutsu."

"What then?" Vance asked, taking another sip of his beer.

Sho's statement about nothing being what it seemed echoed in his mind.

"Good question. Old style Japanese Jujutsu maybe. The sword stuff is kenjutsu. Samurai shit."

"How do you know it's not ninjutsu?"

"I did a ton of research on the ninja and let me tell you, they're hard to pin down. I have no doubt that you studied some school or a hybrid school of old style Japanese martial arts, but the shinobi were so secretive not much is known about them. They were, from what I understand, intelligence gatherers and guerrilla soldiers.

"Some think the ninja were a subdivision of the samurai. In the 1970s Japan had a thing called Ninja-Mania, and the states had their own in the 1980s. It all became very lucrative. Ninja dojo opened all over the place. Many martial arts teachers, no matter the art or style, wanted to stake a claim to the fame and the money. That doesn't mean there were no true teachers. There were some in Japan, but even there the art is controversial. What I'm saying is, everything is suspect. Look, even the stone padlocks they gave you to use are *Ishi Sashi*. Old-school Okinawan karate training."

"So, Sho lied about being a ninja?"

"Sho might not be lying. He could be repeating what his teacher told him. Japanese students don't question."

"So, I've heard," Vance said, recalling the conversation with Kevin. He pushed the thought of Kevin from his mind. He didn't need emotion or his own failures distracting him.

"Anyway, these ninjutsu instructors, to my mind are teaching a reconstruction of ninjutsu. It's like reenacting the Civil War or the American Revolution. Many Japanese see it this way. Most modern arts only go back a hundred years. So, it's not that big a deal anyway."

"Wouldn't Sho know what he's teaching isn't completely authentic?" Vance asked. "He's Japanese."

"We'll get to that in a minute," Murphy said. "The point is, everything you told me over the phone, all the techniques that you practiced are just good old regular karate, jujutsu, aikido, and Judo with some ninja seasoning."

"Did he invent this 'ninja seasoning' as you call it?" Vance asked.

"No, it's been pulled from elsewhere. Modern Japanese construction workers wear tabi boots. They're not ancient. The shujenja practice comes from Yamabushi priests. Kuji-in is from Mikkyo Buddhism. Ninja stars weren't even used by the ninja back in their day. It's a modern association created to protect the image of the samurai, who were the ones who actually used them. I could go on. Suffice it to say, Sho's ninjutsu is a hodgepodge of a lot of cool stuff. But true ninjutsu, an unbroken lineage, it ain't."

"But he showed me the *densho* scrolls that were passed on in his family," Vance said, not wanting to believe it.

"Can you read Japanese? Didn't think so. Even if they are true shinobi scrolls, they're easily purchased legally. Doesn't mean he has the authority of the ryu or school to teach, though."

"That's all very disappointing," Vance said.

"It gets worse," Murphy said. "That Cell Block Shuffle prison fighting system is an urban myth."

"I was taught how to shank someone," Vance said leaning in and lowering his voice. *I almost shanked someone*, Vance thought, not wanting to think it.

"Shanking is real," Murphy said. "The system? Not so much."

"So, I've been played?"

Steve returned with their order, all the food steaming hot in metal serving dishes: shrimp fried rice, moo shu pork, beef and broccoli, and a tidbit appetizer plate. Polynesian style. Vance's favorite.

Murphy ordered another bourbon, and Vance another beer.

Steve left them to their conversation, returning to the adjacent family to light the Sterno for their pu-pu platter. The children looked in awe at the blue flame as it danced and crackled.

"I'll tell you this, though," Murphy said, as he scooped rice from a metal serving dish. "You're in deep shit."

Vance sighed. Trying to keep his hand steady, he spread the *Hoisin* sauce and spooned the meat and vegetable mix onto the *moo shu* pancake.

Murphy made his own, took a bite, before wiping his hands on a cloth napkin. He grabbed a file folder decorated in Post-It notes scribbled in Murphy's illegible handwriting.

"It's a good thing you called me. I didn't tell you I was a private investigator by trade. Not supposed to anyway."

"So, you're not in sales?" Vance asked with a wink.

"Yeah, I know you knew something was up. Let's go through Shoto Maramoto's background. He was born in the good ol' US of A—California. San Fran. Most likely lived in an internment camp as a child during World War Two.

"His background is fuzzy. Got involved with organized crime at a young age—Japanese American wannabees, not true Yakuza. He has all his fingers. They like to take those for infractions. The real Yakuza threw him and his gang off their turf. Ended up in Rhode Island. Probably needed to go cross-country to keep his fingers or his life. Carved out some action in the Ocean State, self-made multi-millionaire."

"I was led to believe Sho was innocent," Vance said. "His son-in-law was covering for him."

"I'll give Sho this," Murphy said. "He's running his organization just like the shinobi of old. Subterfuge and middlemen. Cut off one head, he still has eight more. He's been investigated for racketeering, assault, bribes, money laundering—the list goes on. This guy's like

Teflon. Sho has multiple warrants out for his arrest, but he's never been charged."

"And that speaks to police corruption," Vance said, remembering how Keikan wanted onto the estate. Keikan couldn't go onto the property without losing his job.

Like a vampire, Keikan had to be invited in. Although, he might turn out to be a beneficial vampire. Once on the property, they would have probable cause to search the estate. Vance felt confident that the police would find plenty of evidence.

Even his money and connections wouldn't keep Sho out of jail this time if that happened. Vance worried that the Kaiden might have kept evidence on him.

"What about Sho's wife?" Vance asked. "Jade's, mother? What happened to her?"

"Fell down the stairs and broke her neck," Murphy said after swallowing a mouthful of food. "I bet dollars to donuts she was pushed."

"What's his motive?" Vance asked.

"Who knows? Could be anything. She could snore too much in her sleep, or she knew too much and he was worried she would become a snitch."

"Great," Vance said, losing his appetite. "What about Detective Keikan?"

"He's on the up and up—all things considered," Murphy said, raising an eyebrow. "Are you ready for this? Keikan legally changed his name."

"What was it?"

"Kudaki Maramoto," Murphy said, proud of the knowledge.

"Holy shit!" Vance said. He looked over at the family beside them. They hadn't noticed. He lowered his voice anyway. "He's Jade's brother?"

"And Sho's son," Murphy said.

"I shouldn't be surprised," Vance said. "It was right there all the time. I just couldn't see it."

"Don't be too hard on yourself, Paladin," Murphy said. "You always see the best in people. Might be a little naive, but I admire that."

"Thanks a lot," Vance said to the backhanded compliment. "Now I have something to tell you. It's going to sound strange."

"Stranger than what you've already told me?"

"Afraid so," Vance said. "What do you know about the tengu."

"I don't know," Murphy said. "Mythical bird men of some sort."

"They're real," Vance said. "Even if Sho isn't a ninja, some of the disciples in his organization can turn into tengu, and oni. I've seen it."

Murphy didn't say anything. He just looked Vance straight in the eyes and blinked.

"You don't believe me?" Vance asked. "Come outside and I'll show you."

"Vance, I believe you," Murphy said. "If you say tengu are real. Then they're real. I know you too well not to believe you. But don't mind if it takes me a minute to wrap my head around all this."

Vance also knew Murphy all too well. This was Murphy's way of dismissing anything he didn't understand. He'd go along to get along, but Vance could feel him trying not to roll his eyes.

Steve returned to clear the table.

"Box whatever's left," Murphy said to Steve. "You paying with cash?"

"I can," Vance said.

"Good man," Murphy said. "I'll need that receipt for my records."

"What's up with that," Vance asked.

"I'm officially on suspension. Don't ask. My boss is cool though. I just need to blow through some petty cash he spotted me. If you get where I'm coming from."

Vance figured he did. Same old Murphy.

Steve brought a bowl of pineapple with toothpicks and two fortune cookies. Vance liked that. Most Chinese restaurants no longer include pineapple with the meal.

Vance stabbed a couple cubes with a toothpick hoping the pineapple would settle his stomach. The acid irritated his tongue.

"If I were you," Murphy said. "I wouldn't go back. Stay at my place for a while. Just don't cramp my style."

"I appreciate the offer," Vance said, breaking open his fortune cookie. "But I need to see this thing through."

"Well, the offer still stands," Murphy said. "Don't hesitate to contact me for any reason. Just be careful. I lost my best friend once. I don't want to go through that again."

Vance nodded. Murphy was a good friend, someone who could be counted on when the chips were down. They shared a bond as strong as family, one that could never be broken.

Vance looked at his fortune and smiled.

It read: *Time to tie up all those loose ends*

Chapter Thirty-Three

Vance returned to the estate feeling slightly uneasy. The guard raised the gate and Vance rolled the Corvette through. The gate closed behind him. He held his breath waiting for the guard to approach. It never happened. Vance just kept on driving. He let out a breath.

After returning the Corvette to the carport, he jaunted up to the mansion.

Upstairs in his room, he sat down and leafed through the file folder Murphy had given him, looking for inspiration.

Maybe he *should* crash on Murphy's couch. He didn't want to end up in prison, or worse. Sho had played him from the start. As much as he didn't want to believe it, the contents of the file bore out Murphy's intel.

Vance didn't want to leave Jade. Like it or not, he'd fallen for her. If he gave up Sho, even to her own brother, she'd hate him forever.

Could he trust Keikan wouldn't put him in a prison cell? He wasn't sure.

He only had one option: confront Sho. He didn't like it.

A knock at the door dispelled any notion of challenging the old man.

Vance suddenly felt weak, as if he had somehow summoned Sho outside his door by thought alone. Could this man read his mind, and his most intimate and treacherous thoughts?

The whole idea seemed ludicrous, but plausible. Anything was possible with Sho. Even if he wasn't a ninja, he still had access to esoteric powers that Vance didn't understand. The hair on the back of his neck and arms stood on end. He hid the file under a couch cushion and opened the door.

"Can I come in?" Jade asked. Dragons on her short silk kimono drew his eyes to bare legs. He forced his gaze back to her face. A face so beautiful in her youth, yet stone behind the smooth exterior. Alabaster.

"Not a good idea," Vance said, stoically. "It's late."

Jade brushed past him. The door closing behind her. Her warmth transferred through the thin garment. He inhaled the subtle scent of cherry blossoms.

Jade untied the robe, let it drop to the floor. Hands on her hips, wearing nothing but a black bra and panties, she struck a haughty pose. The lingerie must be courtesy of Gorflands.

She moved closer and embraced him. Her velvet lips pressed against his, tasted her sweet warm breath and tongue. The warmth of her body saturated through his clothing. Arousal overcame him. His body ached.

He wanted to make love to her, let all thoughts of Sho, of prison, of tengu, of doing the right thing vanish. Regaining his senses, he gently pushed her away.

"Jade, I can't. I…." Vance said, searching for words that would not come.

He had gone against his own ethics many times while staying on the estate, why couldn't he do this?

She blinked away tears. Her faux green eyes sparkled unnaturally. Anger overtook her expression.

Her reaction reinforced what he already knew: all her anger, all her bluster, all her haughtiness was a mask that hid the vulnerable girl inside.

It had taken all her courage to attempt this seduction. She had faced and conquered her fear of rejection. But now that he had indeed rejected her, the walls of false strength crumbled, showing him the real young woman underneath, a woman that he thought he could love for the rest of his life.

Silently, she reclaimed her kimono, tied it closed, and stormed out.

Vance stood in shocked silence. Then rushed out into the hallway.

Empty.

He imagined her a phantom disappearing in a puff of smoke and billowing fog.

Vance stood silently in the empty hall. He didn't know what to do and couldn't muster the energy to chase her. Returning to his room alone seemed a terrible burden.

A strange feeling overcame him, a feeling of being watched. His eyes searched every nook but could see no one. He couldn't identify anything that might be a camera.

Reluctantly, and with mixed emotions, he returned to his room to plan his next move.

Vance contemplated everything from a run around the grounds of the estate, to expend pent up energy, to a cold shower, to snuff out the burning desire within.

A knock at the door.

If he answered, and it was Jade, he wouldn't be able to resist a second time.

What if it were Sho? What would he say? He didn't have an answer.

Tentatively, he opened the door. This time, a faux blue-eyed girl stood before him. A short black dress hugging an athletic figure.

"Sapphire?"

She placed a finger over his lips and gently pushed him inside.

"I saw Jade visit you," she said, a sly smile brightening her face.

"You know I wouldn't…." Vance said.

"I know," Sapphire said, so close he could not control his arousal. "But you wanted to. Eventually you'll give in—no matter how pure your intentions."

He wanted to contradict her but couldn't. She had seen his true face, as he had seen hers. The Hyde underneath the Jekyll.

"What happened to the Kaiden?" Vance asked, as a distraction.

"I'm not here to talk about the Kaiden," Sapphire said, hiking up her dress.

Pulling his hand down, Vance felt her warm nakedness. Touching her gently, she moaned. His erection was now painful.

"Transform, Vance," Sapphire said seductively. "Be what you are."

Why was she acting this way? He didn't care, couldn't think. They removed their clothing and transformed. Turning her around and bending her over, Vance freed himself and entered her. Her warmth enveloped him.

Sapphire gasped.

They hovered. Their wings fluttered, holding them aloft.

Sapphire orgasmed. Her moans released his floodgates. He erupted, gritting his teeth.

The act completed, they returned to human form once more.

For the first time, he could truly believe the demon inside had been released.

The front door opened.

"Are you in here, Vance? I wanted to apologize--"

Jade stopped mid-sentence. She had changed into a pair of jeans and a sweater.

"Oh, my God," Vance said.

Jade's eyes watered. Mouth agape. Then she ran.

Vance and Sapphire rushed after her.

How could he be so stupid? How could he have given in to temptation?

Once outside, Sapphire grabbed Vance, turning him around.

"Where are you going?"

"The carport."

"We don't need a car," Sapphire said.

"I'm not changing again," Vance said. "I'm done."

"You're anything but done," Sapphire said. "Come on."

At the carport, an empty parking space stood in place of Jade's bike.

Vance slid into the Corvette. Sapphire jumped into the passenger side.

They sped off. The guard opened the gate. Vance made a split-second decision. Turned right.

No matter if she were headed to downtown Newport or Providence, she'd have to go in that direction.

"Where would she go?" Vance asked, speaking his thoughts.

"Where do girls her age go when they're upset?"

"You tell me," Vance said, aggravated. "You have more experience with that than I do."

Sapphire didn't answer.

He only hoped they'd find her quickly.

Chapter Thirty-Four

"Why are we back on stakeouts?" Hayden asked. It had only taken him a few days to make the inquiry. At least Hayden was developing more patience. Hayden and Keikan sat in the darkness of the Crown Vic, the motor off.

"That's my little surprise for you," Keikan said. "You'll know it when you see it."

"I don't get it," Hayden said, rubbing the stubble on his chin. "Why don't you grab Vance before he goes inside."

"I told you. I have a better idea."

He couldn't see Vance letting him on the estate. Not without some type of leverage. Vance would be loyal to Sho, even if it went against his own best interest. That's who Vance was. It spoke to his character. Keikan understood Vance's convictions. They were admirable.

Keikan needed Vance. Sho would hole up in the estate for the rest of his life. He knew Sho couldn't leave for multiple reasons.

Keikan said a silent prayer. He needed a break, a small miracle so he could find a way to stop Sho before more people got hurt. Keikan felt a solemn duty to stop him.

As if his prayer had been answered, a rider on a motorcycle pulled out and took off down the darkened street.

"That's her!" Keikan said slapping the dashboard. "Let's go!"

Without hesitation, Hayden pulled onto the road, crossing the median, and giving chase.

"Who's her?" Hayden said, putting his foot down on the gas and flicking on his grill lights and siren.

"Jade," Keikan said. "My sister."

"What's going on, Keikan?" Hayden asked, but he kept up the pursuit.

Keikan gave him the short version. It was a risk. Hayden might not want any part of it.

"Are you in?" Keikan asked.

"Yeah, I'm in," Hayden said. "I couldn't get into any more trouble if I tried. Hopefully, your lady friend will feel the same."

Kekian hadn't planned on giving Stacy the full story. Truthfully, he hadn't even thought about it. Maybe honesty was best. He'd have to think on it.

Jade looked back at them, glancing over her shoulder, and then hit the throttle.

Hayden gave chase, following as Jade weaved in and out of traffic. The blue and whites strobing over her and the bike. Lit against the darkness, Newport Bridge loomed in the distance.

Crossing his fingers, Keikan pulled out his cell with the other hand and made the call.

Even though the older model car had been souped up for duty use, Keikan knew they didn't have a prayer of catching her. They also didn't have a chopper at their disposal. So, keeping tabs on her from the air was out. Once Jade was out of view, there would be no following her. He had to anticipate her next move. He hoped he already had.

Up ahead, well out of reach of Hayden's Vic, Jade turned onto the first exit ramp before the bridge.

"That's it, we've lost her," Hayden said.

"We'll see," Keikan said, feeling tension throughout his body.

Hayden pulled onto the exit. A Newport Patrol car sat jackknifed, blocking the off ramp, boxing her in.

Jade would have been long gone but she hadn't attempted to make a getaway by driving over the grassy median for two obvious reasons.

First, Keikan figured she wasn't confident enough to pull such a risky move for fear of crashing the bike and getting herself killed. She wasn't wearing a helmet, either.

Second, Officer Stacy Pepper stood in an isosceles stance, her weapon trained on Jade. Keikan couldn't remember a time Stacy looked better wearing her duty blues.

Chapter Thirty-Five

"We're never going to find her," Vance said. They were driving aimlessly through the narrow streets of downtown Newport. Jade could be anywhere. *Had she headed to Providence?* He couldn't be sure. He didn't think she'd go back to the rave building.

His phone rang.

You have a phone?" Sapphire asked, brows raising, as if he carried some sort of contraband.

"Vance," he said answering the call.

"Vance, this is Detective Keikan."

"What's up?" Vance asked, his heart sinking.

"Looking for Jade?" Keikan said.

"I am."

"I'm holding Jade for speeding, reckless driving, and resisting arrest," Keikan said. "I'd like to return her to you."

"What do you want?" Vance asked, ignoring Sapphire's worried stare.

Keikan told him.

"Why?"

"My real name is Kudaki Maramoto," he said.

"I already figured that out," Vance said.

"Then you know the story. I'm trying to save Jade's life. Get her away from Sho—from my father."

"You're asking a lot," Vance said, his temples aching.

"Here's something else you should know: you were declared legally dead. That status hasn't changed."

"What?"

"You're a man who doesn't exist. You become a loose end, you disappear and nobody's the wiser. Hear what I'm saying? I promise you this: you help me, I'll make sure you don't do time. You'll get your life back. I might even be able to send a little money your way. Enough to allow you to start over. You'll also be doing your duty by protecting Jade."

"I can't talk," Vance said. "Stay by the phone."

He ended the call and dropped the phone into his jacket pocket.

"What was that about?" Sapphire asked, blue eyes piercing.

"Jade's brother," Vance said, a hand now free to rub his temples.

"Shit," Sapphire said. "We need a plan of action. It's time to reactivate the Kaiden."

"Forget the Kaiden," Vance said. "It's time to talk to Sho."

Chapter Thirty-Six

Murphy returned to his apartment, grabbed a beer from the fridge, and sat down in front of the tube. He surfed until landing on a local news channel.

A knot formed in his stomach when the anchor announced the story. As the station went to a live shot, Murphy turned up the volume.

"We're on the scene at the Framingham home of Robert Donovan, a former police officer who had been the current Investigations Manager for Crusader Security in Westborough.

"Donovan was gunned down this evening in his driveway, in what some police officers are calling a gangland hit. Investigators are still struggling to piece together the events. If you look behind me, you'll see the police have cordoned off his suburban home...."

Murphy shut off the TV. He sat in silence, trying to digest the information. Donovan's murder couldn't be a coincidence. Murphy had learned there were few coincidences in his line of work.

The next problem: would someone come looking for him? Murphy found it unlikely. They hadn't abducted and tortured Donovan for information. Instead, they killed him to send a message. That message had come through loud and clear.

He needed to contact Vance. It was worse than he had thought.

Vance was in terrible danger.

Chapter Thirty-Seven

"We should see Sho together," Sapphire said as they returned the Corvette to its parking spot."

"I want to talk to him alone," Vance said, shutting down the vehicle. Silence surrounded them.

"Be careful, Vance," she said. "You have a lot of questions. I don't think you're going to like the answers."

"I'm sure I won't," Vance said, under his breath.

"Just don't become a traitor," Sapphire said, her eyes narrowing before exiting the vehicle and walking toward the mansion alone.

He followed well behind, allowing her to enter first.

Returning to his room, Vance pulled out the burner phone and made a call. The time for discretion had ended.

Keikan answered.

Vance gave him instructions, ended the conversation, and then made another call.

Murphy answered.

"Hey, I was just about to go find you," Murph said. "My informant is dead. You better get out of there."

"Too late for that, Murph," Vance said, filling him in.

"How can I help?" Murphy asked without missing a beat.

"Got any friends who like to kick ass?" Vance asked.

"I can scrounge a couple."

"Thanks, Murph," Vance said. "I'm counting on the cavalry."

Chapter Thirty-Eight

Keikan, Hayden, and Pepper waited on Mill Street across from Touro Park.

Jade remained locked in the backseat of Pepper's cruiser.

The park lights lit Newport Tower, also known as the Old Stone Mill, turning it into a beacon of sorts. A remnant from another age.

The origins of the circular stone tower, with its arched column base, were a mystery. One controversial theory suggested that the Knights Templar had constructed it on an ancient trip to New England, almost a hundred years before Columbus set sail for the New World.

Keikan liked that theory. Fact or fiction, it spoke to his romantic side. He also found it apropos—he was on his own crusade, of sorts.

A little to the right stood the statue of William Ellery Channing, a famous Unitarian Universalist Minister. The copper sculpture now green with age.

A black police SUV pulled up and parked in the wrong direction. Lieutenant Love, Patel-Morran, Finnegan, and Anderson exited the vehicle.

"Thanks for coming," Keikan began. "I appreciate your loyalty. It's time you all learn about my past."

He gave them a rundown in a succinct yet dispassionate fashion. He wasn't one to mix emotions with business. Although he wanted to, he didn't remove the fantastical parts. They had to know what they were dealing with.

"Now that you know, if you want to leave, I won't hold you here."

Nobody moved.

"I didn't get into this job to play it safe," Love said, breaking the tension. Everyone nodded.

"You believe everything I told you?"

"No. But we know you're not nuts," Love said. "At least not any crazier than us. Look what we brought you."

They had filled the back of the SUV full of riot gear: helmets with ballistic face shields and tactical body armor. Basically, 21st century kendo armor. Next to it lay a pile of Remington 870 Police Magnum tactical pump shotguns.

"Rubber bullets, beanbag rounds, and flash bangs are the order of the day," Keikan said. "We're taking Sho with a minimum of collateral damage. If everything goes south, we'll load up lethal. Let's stay safe."

"I'm not dressed for the party. Too old to be encumbered," Hayden said, brushing his tweed jacket. "But I'd still like to come along."

"I appreciate it," Keikan said, giving him a pat on the shoulder. He had grown to like Hayden, even his curmudgeonly side. "I have something to do before suiting up."

Chapter Thirty-Nine

Vance found Sho sitting behind his desk in the study. A tengu mask hung on the wall behind Sho. It was like looking in a mirror. In that mask, Vance saw his true face.

The door stood open. So, he walked in without so much as a courtesy knock. He was all out of courtesy.

"We need to talk, Sho," Vance said.

"Do we, Mr. Palladian?" Sho asked, annoyed at the interruption. He closed his laptop, folded his hands over the cover, and cocked his head.

Then Vance noticed them. He gasped.

The covers had been removed from the busts, and now he knew why they had looked so human.

"Do you like them, Mr. Palladian?" Sho asked, grinning wickedly.

"They're ghoulish," Vance said, feeling his hackles rise.

The dust covers removed, two headless torsos stood on either side of the room, held aloft by steel wire connected to a metal base.

"They were Yakuza," Sho said. "Their full body tattoos expertly preserved. They're not legal to buy or possess...."

"But you don't care what's legal," Vance said, anger rising.

"A man with true power defines his own life," Sho said. "Makes his own laws."

"That's why you're trapped here on this estate," Vance said, watching Sho's expression turn bitter.

"No, there's another reason. One that you can't fathom."

"I'm sure I can't, " Vance said. He didn't have time for Sho's games. "There's something you need to know."

"Go on," Sho said.

"Kudaki has Jade," Vance said.

"What?" Sho said, standing up.

"Or should I call him Christian Keikan?" Vance said, holding his ground. "Keikan called me a few minutes ago. He interrogated me the day I played bodyguard to Jade. I didn't tell him anything because of my loyalty to the Kaiden, and to you. I thought Kevin was protecting you with his criminal activities. But your son says you are the real criminal, and you've been playing me."

"You want the whole truth, Mr. Palladian?" Sho asked.

"Nothing but," Vance said.

"Good. Then let's end this charade," Sho said, unbuttoning his shirt to reveal a scrawl of green and black tattoos that symbolized Yakuza affiliation. Sho's body appeared in great condition for a man his age, strengthened by a lifetime of intense training. "I do not feel compelled to follow the laws of a society that dropped two atomic bombs on Japan and put its own citizens in internment camps.

"Kudaki strayed from the family. Gave up his birthright. He wanted to be a police officer. I thought it was just teenage rebellion, but something was wrong with his mind. He became completely obsessed with taking Jade away from me."

"Can you blame him?" Vance asked.

"Yes, yes I can, Mr. Palladian," Sho said. "Jade is here of her own free will. She can leave anytime. I sent you out to protect her, not keep her a prisoner. And you've failed in your duties. In ancient times you would commit *seppuku*, ritual suicide, to restore your honor."

"We're not in ancient times," Vance said, but he felt shame. He *had* failed Jade, and he had failed himself. He didn't care one wit about Sho. "And you're not a ninja. You're not even a Yakuza. Just an old man playing pretend."

"I am how I define myself," Sho said, standing up straighter. "And I define myself as a sorcerer. I'm stuck on this estate not because I fear arrest but because of a magic ritual that has given me earthly wealth and power at a price. I must remain on this estate. My powers are rooted to the land. I made you a great warrior through my version of the World War Two *Rikugun Nakano Gakko,* spy school and gave you the powers of the tengu. Have I not successfully headed my own organization? I have, like the *jonin,* ninja leaders of old, been running the show the whole time with you unaware. Kevin was just a middleman. He took all his orders from me. You didn't complain while you were enjoying my hospitality—or Sapphire."

"Sapphire?" The revelation knocked the wind out of him. Although, it shouldn't have been a surprise.

"Yes. I sent her to your room. Like the *kunoichi,* female ninja agents of ancient Japan, she's trained in the art of pleasing men, and if necessary, teasing out needed information. You'd like to see her again, eh? I can arrange that."

Vance tried to put Sho's words out of his mind.

"Why am I still legally dead?"

"You're a man who doesn't exist. A shadow. A specter. A true kaiden. A tengu! In my organization, you can do what no other man can."

"And you can kill me with no one ever knowing I was still alive."

"You're more valuable to me alive than dead. I didn't lie about my vision. I still believe you will save my daughter. Jade believes this as well."

"What really happened at the convenience store?" Vance asked.

"You're very astute. I originally saw you in a newspaper article in the *Providence Journal.* The man they called the Paladin—a martial arts instructor. After reading the article, I knew you were the one. We staged the convenience store robbery. You know that already. What you don't know is that Jade was in on it."

Vance involuntarily gasped.

Sho's smile turned sinister.

"Haven't you figured it out yet? An Oni didn't hit you with a baseball bat. Jade jabbed you with a needle, injected you with a drug that put you into a coma. I paid off an administrator and some staff to keep you asleep for a year. Who knows? Maybe I even had your wife killed. Taking away your old life made you easier to recruit."

"You son of a bitch," Vance said, stepping forward. He wanted to kill this man, and martial arts master or not, he'd do it.

Sho moved his hands in a flourish. Smoke billowed around him. Did he have this power or was it some sort of trick?

"Think before you act, Mr. Palladian," Sho said from behind the haze. "Your old life is over. You belong with us. Your training, transformation, as well as your leadership skills, puts you in perfect position to lead the Kaiden. It's your destiny."

"Damn you, Sho!" Vance screamed.

The smoke dissipated. Vance stood alone in the study.

Sho had become a phantom who moved through the world ephemeral.

Chapter Forty

Keikan made his way across Touro park to Channing Memorial Unitarian Universalist Church.

"Are you a priest?" Keikan asked a man locking up for the night.

"I'm a minister," the man said. He had a kind way about him that spoke of a gentle soul. "We're a Unitarian church. Very different from a Catholic church."

"I'm a cop," Keikan said, flashing his badge. "I need a blessing, and a chance to make a confession before a dangerous arrest tonight."

"I don't know...." the minister said, indecision colored his face. "I'm not a Catholic priest."

"Please," Keikan said. "I need your help."

The minister thought for a moment. The silence maddening.

"Well, Detective," the minister finally said. "You're in luck. I was raised Catholic and confirmed. Come inside. I'll do my best."

The minister led Keikan into the Gilded Age church. He snapped the lights on. They navigated the aisle toward the nave. The minister directed Keikan to sit in the front pew.

"Feel free to pray while I prepare."

Keikan took a deep breath and cleared his mind. The effigy of his lord and savior absent, he still felt like he had walked into a house of God. Although, he missed the somber Roman Catholic ascetic, which characterized that expression of the faith. It lent weight to repentance, a visceral quality that pushed down on him, as if God had added weight and mass to the proceedings.

In his own adopted church, he liked to arrive in-between services when the pews lay empty, and he could sit and pray.

He believed that to God everything in the world was mundane. If everything was mundane, then nothing was off limits in prayer.

Although, all prayer, all the prayers in the world couldn't divert God's will.

Hadn't God sacrificed his only begotten son for his people?

God had made sacrifices in creating the world and would continue to make them in accordance with His will.

He bowed his head and clasped his hands together and prayed.

"Lord," he said in a whisper. "I'm here to do your work. Thank you for protecting and guiding me. I know we must all sacrifice for what is right, just as you sacrificed your life for us. All I ask is for the courage to act, and to be victorious in sacrifice."

The minister returned and, acting as priest, heard Keikan's confession, forgave him of his sins. Keikan said five Our Fathers and three Hail Mary's as penitence.

The minister placed his hand on Keikan's head.

"St. Michael the Archangel. Defend and guide your humble servant in his duties to serve and protect the people of his city and state."

Then the minister dipped his finger into a small bowl filled with water he'd blessed and drew a cross on Keikan's forehead.

"I bless you in the name of the Father, the Son, and the Holy Spirit. Amen."

Keikan crossed himself.

Done, he thanked the minister, leaving the church to fulfill his mission and meet his destiny—whatever it might be.

Chapter Forty-One

Vance slipped out of the mansion. In the darkness, the estate looked like a ghost town. It wouldn't stay that way long.

Barely breathing hard from his run, Vance reached his destination.

At the carport, Vance started the Corvette and headed out.

As he approached, the gate remained shut.

The guard sprung from the shack; gun drawn.

Nothing like projecting your intentions. Hadn't Sho taught this guy anything?

Vance hit the gas, engine roar drowning out the guard's screams.

The guard didn't shoot. He didn't need to shoot.

Plowing through the reinforced barrier would be suicide. The car would crumple like tinfoil. For Sho, it would solve the problem.

Vance braced for impact.

At the last second, he pulled the emergency brake.

The Corvette spun 180 degrees. A thud as the car hit the guard, launching him.

Vance stomped the brakes, threw the shifter into park, and jumped out of the vehicle.

Dazed, the guard got to his feet. Unarmed but angry, he was clearly ready for a fight.

Vance traversed the distance, muscle memory taking over. Launching a hook kick, he whipped it old school over his opponent's shoulder, crashing his heel into the guard's jaw.

The guard dropped.

Then it was time for new school. Ground and pound!

Vance crouched, launching three cement-smashing punches, knocking out the guard. Old school Tae Kwon Do mixed with new school MMA. He was back, baby!

Patting the guard down, Vance retrieved a pair of zip-ties from a belt pouch. He used them to easily restrain the guard.

The guard's gun had been knocked out of his hands and swallowed by the night. There was no time to go searching. Vance didn't have the training to use it anyway. But it would have provided a small comfort.

Hefting the guard into a firefighter's carry, Vance deposited him with a thud onto the floor of the shack. Finding the control panel, he pressed the button to lift the gate. The iron barrier slowly rose.

Underneath the control panel he located wires, grabbed hold, and pulled them out. Sparks flew and smoke billowed. He pressed the button again. Nothing happened. The gate was disabled.

Keikan and Murphy would have no problem getting in now.

Things were going to play out quickly; he could feel it in the racing of his heart.

His phone buzzed.

A text from Keikan.

What in the hell?

Maybe Keikan understood something he didn't. After all, Keikan had lived on the estate for years. Vance would have to trust him.

Vance followed Keikan's orders and made off toward the texted destination.

Chapter Forty-Two

Hayden and Keikan roared through the open gates in the Crown Vic, the Black SUV following, and Pepper's cruiser, with Jade in the back, taking up the rear position.

Keikan felt strange returning to the estate. It was like stepping into a memory. Even at night, he could see the grounds hadn't changed since he left.

"Vance Palladian is a man of his word," Hayden said, as they drove up the access road toward the mansion. "I'll give him that."

Keikan picked up the mic. They had turned radios to an alternative channel to thwart anyone monitoring them with a scanner.

If he had had more manpower, Keikan would have surrounded the estate. No doubt some of Sho's staff would slip away, along with Kaiden members. For the Kaiden, he'd need helicopters in the air. Even then, he didn't know how a pilot would react if the Kaiden decided to take to the air. Sho would stay. He had no choice. His powers were tied to the land, and the tengu powers were tied to Sho. For Sho, this would be his last stand. He was sure of it.

"All quiet on the western front," Keikan said into the mic. "Keep your eyes open. We're being watched."

Where the hell was Vance? He needed confirmation of his invitation as a political shield. That could mean the difference between keeping and losing his job.

His smartphone buzzed and displayed a text message.

Meet me at Teahouse Dojo. You and Jade. Vance.

That was strange. Why the dojo? Why not make the exchange right here?

"Vance wants me to bring Jade to the Teahouse," Keikan said, pointing at the shadowy structure in the distance.

"Sounds crazy," Hayden said.

"It gets crazier. Lots of open ground."

"Sniper's paradise," Hayden said.

Keikan nodded but didn't believe his dad wanted to end that way. Sho had something else planned, he knew it.

Chapter Forty-Three

Sho made his way through the secret passage that led from his study to what he liked to call the oval room, a space decorated with antique furniture and baroque paintings. Walking through walls was not within his ability. Sometimes illusion would have to suffice. Sapphire awaited him.

"Vance is off the rails," Sho said.

"I know," Sapphire said. Her expression remained aloof, unreadable.

"The end is near for this estate," Sho said. "They are going to make arrests."

"We have contingency plans," Sapphire said. We already eliminated the former cop who was asking around about you."

"Good."

"The Kaiden and our soldiers stand ready to protect you," Sapphire said.

"I will not leave without Jade," Sho said. "You know that. I'm prepared to do whatever is necessary to get Jade back."

"We can't lose you. You're too valuable." Sapphire said. "We'll get you to a new location."

"No need. I've already arranged for everything. Vance will return to us when Kudaki is dead. Then we can start again."

"What is your command?" Sapphire asked. Sho knew she wouldn't like it.

Sho had no problem with Sapphire acting as leader of the Kaiden temporarily. He trusted her to do so. For the long haul, he needed

Vance to take over. Vance alone could fill the vacuum left by Kevin's death. Vance was charismatic, a natural leader. And his most secret desire would be his undoing. It would allow Sho to scrub him of his paladin identity forever.

Sapphire nodded reluctantly, transformed from a woman into a demon, and walked away to do what she must do.

Sho removed a painting from the wall, revealing a combination safe. He entered the pass code and removed a passport, an LED headlamp, a small stack of cash, and a sub-compact pistol stowed in a covert holster.

He might have been tied to the estate through the spell that had been inked on his back, but that would be easily if painfully removed by fire. The Kaiden and the oni would lose all their abilities, their powers. He would heal, re-ink, and start again.

He dropped the passport into his shirt pocket, clipped the money into his billfold, and strapped on the headlamp. Then he removed the gun, tucking the leather holster under his arm. Depressing the magazine release, he found it fully stacked with 9mm ammunition. He pushed the mag back into the ammo well. It clicked into place, telling him it had seated. Then he racked the slide, loading a round into the chamber. He had plenty of surprises in store. For everyone.

Sho clipped the holstered gun to the inside of his waistband. Then he sent a text message.

Removing a larger painting revealed an opening in the wall, and a stairwell. Turning on the headlamp, he descended. At the bottom he bent over and entered a cramped concrete tunnel. His back ached, and his knees protested. His footfalls echoed through the darkness and the dampness chilled the air.

Even though in good shape for his years, he still found the journey laborious. Panting and sweating, despite cool surroundings, he kept going.

My willpower will survive even my death.

Exiting the tunnel, he allowed a moment to catch his breath and stretch his back, before descending another set of steps to a dank rocky area.

He could now see an opening, and the subtle brightness of evening. The scent of fresh water revitalized him. He trudged on.

Sho emerged through the cave in the back of the waterfall.

His next steps were clear. He would first traverse all the way to the woods where he had taken Vance hunting. Then he would make his way surreptitiously across the estate, the night as his cover, to what he hoped would be the final confrontation.

Chapter Forty-Four

Vance waded through the darkness of the estate toward his destination. His first encounter with Sho seemed so long ago. So much had happened since he had begun this journey. Now he was totally in over his head. Barely treading water. He just wanted this to be over. When he reached the dojo, he looked over his shoulder. Nothing stirred under the blanket of darkness that had been pulled over the estate. He climbed the steps and entered, closing the door behind him.

Out of habit, and ingrained reverence, he bowed, but this time didn't kick off his shoes.

"Hello," he said to the empty dojo. Snapping on the lights dispelled all shadows. Nowhere for anyone to hide.

He closed the door behind him and walked to the center of the dojo unsure of what to do next.

"Welcome back to your training, Mr. Palladian," Sho said behind him.

Vance whirled around, hands up, ready to fight. The estate had too many buildings with secret doors.

Sho trained his pistol on Vance.

"I'm really getting sick of your parlor tricks," Vance said, but fear gripped him. "What are you gonna do?"

"It's not what I'm going to do, Mr. Palladian. You're going to fulfill the prophecy," Sho said. "You're going to save my daughter."

Chapter Forty-Five

Keikan exited the Vic, took a breath, and looked around. The estate was too still and too quiet. The guard shack stood abandoned.

Electricity in the air, pressure building as from a storm in the distance. His neck hair bristled. He needed to act quickly.

He nodded at his team ready in the SUV.

Pepper powered down the passenger window as he approached.

"I'll take Jade," Keikan said, and gave Pepper instructions. "Push comes to shove. Get the hell away. Nothing is worth your life."

Pepper smiled, his concern making her eyes misty. Keikan pretended not to notice.

"This won't end well for you, big brother," Jade said, eyes radiating hate.

Grabbing her arm, Keikan helped her from the vehicle. Truthfully, he didn't expect any of this to go well. Sho had trained her well enough that even in handcuffs, she was dangerous.

Sapphire, in tengu form, lay in wait with a well-trained group of oni soldiers in the darkened woods just beyond the guardhouse. Sho had trained this contingent in archery. Wearing woodland camouflage shirts and trousers, with tabi to match, they blended invisibly into the forest.

As the first line of defense, they would assault the intruders with silent projectiles. Without noise, the outside world would never know a war raged inside the estate, and no reinforcements would come.

Law enforcement had been militarized to combat terrorism but could as easily bring that force to bear on the Kaiden.

Sapphire knew that one day she might have to pay for her crimes, but she was determined today would not be that day. The Kaiden and the oni soldiers had been given a Plan B, and she had her own.

Waiting, and watching she couldn't help but wonder what would become of Vance. Would he survive? And if so, would he ever return to the Kaiden? She tried to push him from her mind, concentrate on the task at hand.

With Kevin gone, Sho had no choice but to put her in charge, a job she had been born to perform. She was more than a sexual weapon in Sho's arsenal, but she knew he didn't see her that way. He was old and steeped in the ancient ways. She was a victim of her own success. Maybe a battle victory would place her in his favor. Wash away the taint of her loyal but lascivious activities.

Three vehicles came into focus as they drove onto the property. They were waiting for something. Perhaps someone. She knew then they were waiting for Vance. Rage filled her. Once this was all over, she would kill him. The traitor deserved no less.

She spied Keikan getting out of a Crown Vic.

"Prepare to fire," she said softly into her lip mike.

She waited until she saw Jade removed from the cruiser.

"Fire!"

Arrow shafts whistled through the air.

A whistling to Keikan's left, from a wooded area beyond the guard shack.

The *thunk* of copper tipped arrows pelted the vehicles, imbedding into the steel side-panels.

"Stay low," Keikan said, pushing Jade toward Hayden's Crown Vic.

Pepper slammed her cruiser into reverse, rocketing through the open gate. Then she spun the vehicle ninety degrees, blocking egress.

Maintaining discipline, Keikan's crew remained in the SUV, holding their fire.

Keikan pushed Jade inside the Vic and slid in next to her.

"Go! Go!" Keikan said.

Hayden punched it.

"Toss the mic."

Hayden lobbed it over his shoulder. Keikan snatched it in midair.

"Douse the lights! Circle the wagons," Keikan said into the mic. "Follow us."

She watched Keikan scramble with Jade to the Vic, watched as the cruiser sped in reverse. Plan A was working.

But once Jade was safely in the Vic, both vehicles made for the mansion.

Shit!

Time for Plan B.

"They're on the move!" Sapphire said into the mic. "Change your battery of arms. You know what to do."

She waited while unseen archers scurried to the mansion.

Sapphire took a deep breath, looked around, and then headed for the carport.

Chapter Forty-Six

Hayden led the SUV clockwise around the circular driveway. The arrow compromised driver's side of the vehicles facing toward the blacked out colonial mansion.

"These motherfuckers are pissing me off," Anderson said, exiting the SUV. "What's with the arrows?"

"They want to scare us off," Keikan said as he approached. Jade remained in the locked vehicle. "They know this is a stealth operation. Too many gunshots will bring in a SWAT team."

Keikan's team assembled behind the cover the SUV provided.

"No more playing around, Keikan," Love said. "They started with arrows. No telling what else they'll throw at us next."

"I already told you we were going in non-lethal."

"That's before we met resistance," Love said. "I can't ask anyone to stay here defenseless. Can you?"

Keikan thought for a moment. He didn't like it.

"Okay," Keikan said. "Load up, but don't engage. Stay covered until I make the exchange and return."

Keikan pulled Hayden to the side.

"Get back in the car and stay there," Keikan said, lowering his voice. "Anything goes down, get your ass gone."

"You know I'm not going anywhere," Hayden said.

"Yeah, I know," Keikan said, resignation coloring his voice. He touched Hayden's shoulder. "Listen, Love can be a hothead. Keep him in line."

"How do I do that?"

"Listen up, everyone," Keikan said, turning back to the team. "Hayden's in charge."

"What?" Love asked, eyes shining with anger.

"What?" Hayden asked, confusion coloring his face.

"Hayden outranks everyone but me," Keikan said. "Something goes down, Hayden calls the shots."

"You're shitting me," Love said, scratching the heat on his neck.

"You don't have to like it," Keikan said.

Love didn't argue. Instead, he loaded his shotgun with live 00 buckshot shells and slugs.

Keikan grabbed a shotgun from the trunk of the Vic, monitoring the upper windows of the mansion. No movement visible.

Keikan helped Jade from the vehicle.

"Let's go," Keikan said. Jade looked at him with loathing in her eyes.

Chapter Forty-Seven

Halfway to the teahouse, the moon peaked out from behind tenebrous clouds. Keikan scanned the shadowy estate. He had forgotten the vastness of his father's empire, and how its tendrils snaked throughout the whole of the Ocean State.

Hayden's quip about sitting ducks for snipers played with his mind. Yet, he didn't believe Sho would resort to that—at least not yet.

Even so, their vulnerability kept him on edge.

Jade slowed just ahead of him.

He pushed her forward with the butt of the shotgun.

She grunted, resuming her pace.

Keikan hated being rough, but time was of the essence. He loved his sister, but he didn't trust her. Not now. Not yet. Sho's influence was still too strong. She'd need years of therapy to erase his brainwashing.

"You're not going to make it out of here alive, big brother," Jade said, looking over her shoulder.

"Just keep moving, Sis," Keikan said. He thought how much safer it would be to knock her out with the butt of his shotgun and fireman carry her over to the dojo. He didn't want to do it, but it certainly was an option.

Her attitude and actions were not wholly her fault. She had been brought up this way.

Who would want an ordinary existence after living in such luxury, not curtailed by laws or authority? A country to oneself. Only a poor bastard like himself.

When they had reached the teahouse, he nudged her forward once again, and they climbed the steps.

Chapter Forty-Eight

Hayden watched through night-vision binoculars as Keikan and Jade entered the teahouse.

Then gunfire erupted from the mansion, muzzle flash blinding in the darkness, peppering the SUV, punching out holes in the side windows. Safety glass shattering, splintering, raining dull shards into the interior.

Looks like they're done with stealth!

Hayden hunkered down as rounds reached his vehicle. He felt rage then.

Getting older meant he couldn't do what he used to do. His body was more brittle. The bones creaked, and the joints swelled from lack of use or yesterday's abuse.

One day, he awakened and found he was a shadow of his younger self. But the anger that burned within restored him. Made him rise from behind the engine block and squeeze the revolver's trigger. The gun bucked to life.

"Nobody fucks with my car!" Hayden screamed. "Open fire!"

Love, Puja, Finnegan, and Anderson fired from behind the SUV.

They had been caught off guard and out gunned—they had only brought close quarter combat weapons. Keikan hadn't anticipated or planned for an all-out battle.

The damn place erupted into a war zone.

Hayden wondered if the sound of gunfire would take the rest of his hearing if it didn't take his life.

The cacophony would bring the cavalry. Hayden just hoped they would arrive in time.

Chapter Forty-Nine

Sapphire made her way stealthily to the carport. She found the Corvette waiting for her. Vance wasn't the only one with a key.

Starting the engine, the dash lights illuminated, showing her that the Corvette had a full tank. That was good. She wouldn't need to stop for fuel until well outside of Rhode Island. She needed to disappear for a while. Execute her own Plan B. If Sho was killed or captured and removed from the estate, she'd lose her power. A vehicle was essential.

Prison wasn't inevitable. She had acquired the paperwork and bank accounts to switch identities and begin a new life.

Sho's organization, while powerful in the Ocean State, didn't have national reach, barely regional. If she didn't return, he didn't have the resources to find her. That is, if he escaped prison. Sho's Teflon coating was wearing thin. Removed from the estate, his powers would wane. His stubbornness would be the end of him.

Sapphire clicked off the lights, shifted the car into drive, and sped down the private road toward freedom.

Approaching the gate, a cruiser blocked her exit.

For an instant, she thought about using the Corvette as a battering ram, hoping the vehicle wouldn't crumple. The impact leaving just enough car to get away.

Those were crazy thoughts. No way would the sports car survive.

A female officer in full riot gear stood behind the cruiser, weapon trained and ready.

The bitch didn't move.

Spinning the wheel to the left, Sapphire stomped on the brakes. The Corvette drifted to a stop sideways, the odor of burned rubber wafting into the cabin.

Chapter Fifty

Officer Stacy Pepper was used to fighting in the ring, but not with her own thoughts. Now, as she waited for all hell to break loose, she battled the demons that had taken up residence in her brain.

Pepper knew this bust could turn into a huge fiasco, get her suspended, even terminated from the force. She'd lose her position in Newport, a plum assignment, and her reputation—if Keikan screwed this up.

For all the strides women had made, it was still difficult for female cops. She had put everything into this career.

Besides mixed martial arts, the only thing she'd ever wanted was to be a cop. How would she transition to a regular job if all went south?

MMA had finally cracked open for women, but she couldn't see making a living at it.

And here she was acting like a schoolgirl with a crush, going along with Keikan and his mad scheme because she liked him. Risking her future for a guy who hardly gave her the time of day.

Keikan was the stoic loaner. A man of mystery that mesmerized her. Was it the challenge she found appealing?

Dating wasn't hard, even with her tomboyish ways, police work, and full contact fighting. Dying an old maid wasn't in the cards. With or without Keikan she could have a satisfying and productive life. She supposed everyone wanted what they couldn't have.

It didn't matter. She was committed, nothing could extricate her now.

Interrupting her thoughts, a black Corvette, no lights, screamed down the roadway, headed straight for her cruiser.

Pepper drew her duty weapon, putting a bead on the vehicle.

Keikan had ordered her to get away. Pepper wasn't built for fleeing. She had taken a beating in the ring, never flinching. Had gone unconscious instead of tapping, putting her life in the hands of her opponent and the referee. She had joined the police force despite opposition from friends and family. She wouldn't back down now.

An instant before she squeezed the trigger, the Corvette skidded sidewise and came to a stop.

Pepper slid over the hood of her cruiser, both hands on her duty weapon, keeping it between herself and the potential threat.

"Keep your hands where I can see them," she screamed. "Out of the car slowly!"

Chapter Fifty-One

Sapphire did as the policewoman commanded. She opened the door slowly. Carefully stepped out of the car, keeping her head down, allowing her peripheral vision to find the female officer's location and judge the distance.

She waited patiently, controlling her breathing as she stepped away from the open door.

As the officer transitioned to a one-handed grip on her duty weapon, Sapphire turned toward the Corvette as if to assume the position.

As she turned, Sapphire whipped her leg out in an inverted round kick, hitting the officer's wrist, creating a hand spasm. The female officer lost her grip on the gun. Dropped it.

Sapphire smiled. It was time to show her true self. Sapphire had her now.

The perp emerged from the vehicle. The woman appeared compliant. She just needed to get her into cuffs.

In a flash of movement, the woman kicked Stacy's gun out of her hand.

Shit!

Then the woman transformed into a demon!

Stacy gasped.

Keikan wasn't lying to her, wasn't putting her on.

With no time to retrieve her backup, a Bond Arms Derringer stowed on her ankle, Stacy prepared for battle. No stranger to contact, she was the defending champion when it came to street altercations. If this blue-eyed demon wanted the title, she'd have to take it.

The demon traversed the distance easily, striking Stacy in the jaw with a *shuto* sword hand. Jarred from the blunt impact, Stacy was unable to defend as the demon wrapped her arm around her back. But Stacy was no Glass Jaw Josie.

Dropping her hips, Stacy countered before the demon could take her into the air, completing a throw.

The demon hit the ground, stomping her feet as she landed to disperse the impact.

Stacy pulled the demon's leathery arm, keeping her from rolling away. Then with a perfect transition, she threaded the demon's arm through her legs, sitting down, completing *Juji Gatame*, a cross arm Judo lock.

She couldn't hold her all day. The demon was struggling. Too strong to restrain.

Fuck it!

Stacy lifted her hips, dislocating the demon's elbow.

The joint gave way and the demon screamed. Even with only one functioning arm, the demon would still be dangerous. Stacy needed to get the cuffs on her. She steeled herself for the effort.

Then a rustling.

Footsteps.

For the second time, Stacy knew she was a goner.

"Shit," a handsome black man said above her. "You just Ronda Rousey-ed the bitch!"

Chapter Fifty-Two

After speaking with Vance, Murphy made some calls. Only two people wanted to get in on the action. Paul Christian Davidson, the student that had brought Vance into the dojo, who had served in Afghanistan, and Steve Chen, the old waiter at the South Pacific Restaurant.

Wouldn't Vance be surprised?

Don't count us out, Murphy thought. *There's enough talent and experience here to give anyone a run for their money.*

Now looking down at the female cop performing Juji Gatame on a female demon, Murphy could do nothing but make a quick quip and shake his head.

"Who are you, guys?" the female cop asked.

"We're the cavalry," Murphy said. "I'm a friend of Vance Palladian."

"Officer Stacy Pepper," she said, still panting from the exertion. "Help me get her into the car."

A volley of gunfire exploded in the distance.

Murphy and his cavalry helped flip the demon over onto her stomach. Despite her protests and screams of pain, Stacy got the cuffs on her.

With the blue-eyed demon returned to human form and stowed safely in the back of the cruiser, Stacy turned to the men.

They were the calvary? She figured Murphy could handle himself, even if his obi belt with *katana* and *wakizashi* clashed with his modern attire, but the old guy in the *kung-fu* pajamas holding *escrima* sticks, and the unarmed younger man, didn't look too formidable to her.

A volley of gunfire erupted from the mansion on the hill.

"You guys don't look prepared for a gunfight."

"Didn't bring one. Don't have a license in your fine state," Murphy said. "But don't worry about us. We're pretty crafty."

Stacy reached into her cruiser and unlatched the Remington.

"Who knows how to handle a shotgun?" she asked.

"I've handled a few in my time," the younger man said. "Military."

"Just be careful," Pepper said as she tossed him the loaded gun. He caught it. "That goes for all of you."

She returned to her patrol vehicle. All those gun shots would eventually alert her comrades in arms. She had no choice but to call dispatch.

Murphy and his team stalked off into the gathering darkness. Slipping to the woods beyond the guard shack, they took a circuitous route to get behind the mansion. Paul took point. He was the only one with military experience.

Navigation was easy, they only had to follow the sound of rifle and shotgun report.

With only a single shotgun between them, the team was majorly outgunned. But it was too late for second thoughts.

Paul led them to the edge of the woods. He held his fist at head level, telling them to freeze. He waited and listened before signaling them forward. Once at a reasonable distance, Paul motioned for them to squat.

From Murphy's vantage point, the back of the mansion appeared unprotected. But he didn't have intel on hidden cameras or boobytraps.

"Do we go forward?" Paul asked in a whisper.

"Let's do it," Murphy said, willing his heart to slow to a normal rhythm. It wasn't working.

Staying low to the ground, they swiftly traversed the clearing and made it to the mansion's backdoor. Steve wasn't even breathing hard. He envied the old bastard.

Paul checked the door. Locked.

"Breach." Murphy said. He and Steve moved out of harm's way.

Paul nodded. Holding the shotgun at a forty-five-degree angle, the muzzle touched the locking mechanism.

Paul fired, splintering wood and dislodging metal.

The door ajar, they readied themselves to enter.

Chapter Fifty-Three

The mansion security command center stood empty, abandoned by Sho's personal security.

A bank of monitors showed the battle playing out in real time.

ROOF NIGHT VISION CAM: A deployment of six demons was firing small arms down at an unseen enemy.

DRIVEWAY NIGHT VISION CAM: A black SUV and an old Crown Vic, windows exploding from gunfire, metal riddled with arrows and bullet holes.

BACK ENTRANCE CAM: Murphy and his crew are stealing inside the mansion, then separating. Each member of Murphy's trio disappeared from camera range.

STAIRWAY 3 CAM: Paul Davidson ascended the stairway with a shotgun pressed against his body.

Back to ROOF NIGHT VISION CAM: Paul Davidson emerged into camera range. He raised his weapon, aimed, and fired. Demons fell like practice targets. This required only three shots of 00 buckshot.

STAIRCASE 1: Steve, the waiter, crept up and entered a room on the second floor.

Over to SPARE ROOM 2ND FL CAMERA: Steve entered the room. A demon turned too late.

Weaving his sticks in a Heaven Six *sinawali* pattern, he knocked the rifle from the demon's hands. The sticks created a soundless percussion, and the demon appeared to spasm. Steve stepped to the side and finished him with a *Juk Tek* Chinese sidekick. The kick knocked the demon out of camera range.

Chapter Fifty-Four

Murphy burst through a door onto a third-floor hallway. A demon, who'd been pacing the hall, whirled around.

Murphy drew his sword and sliced through a demon with one sure motion. Then Murphy skipped in, throwing a Tae Kwon Do sidekick, breaking ribs and knocking the demon through a banister, splintering wood.

More demons entered from a room on the left. He raised his sword and ran toward them screaming a terrifying *kiai*, spirit shout.

Cutting down with the katana, unable to hear their screams over his own, he lost count of demons killed. Warm blood splattered his face.

An explosion of pain as he's slammed into a wall. His bloody katana clattered across marble flooring.

A massive white tengu with a skeleton face, and another with a golden one, stared down at him.

The large tengu picked him up and slammed him into the wall, breaking through to the studs. A plume of plaster coated him. The white skull grinned through powdery smoke.

Murphy shook his head—plaster flying—regaining his senses. The pain receded.

He hadn't imagined the fight going like this. His ass is being handed to him. The demon could lodge him deep into the wall, making it his permanent resting place, at least until they brought an excavation team in to reach him.

Screw that!

Cupping his hands, Murphy slapped below the big motherfucker's horns, creating suction, blowing out his eardrums.

The massive tengu screamed, blood trickling from his ears. The tengu jerked and tossed him. Murphy felt the sensation of weightlessness. Rounding his body, he hit the floor, performed a back roll. The ukemi absorbed most of the impact. Yet, his back and shoulder still ache. Marble floors have no give.

The big tengu dropped to his knees but was still conscious. He was one tough mother. The blow should have knocked him out. Then he's not a tengu any longer, just a strong Samoan.

Now it's the smaller tengu's turn to dance.

"Hey, asshole!" It's Steve, emerging from the second floor.

The gold tengu turned to greet him, assuming a combat stance.

Steve weaved his sticks into a whirlwind. Murphy now understood why some Filipino stick fighting traditions called their art Kali, after the multi-armed Hindu goddess of death and destruction.

The tengu whipped out a *manriki gusari*, weighted chain. *Where'd he get that?*

In one quick motion, the chain struck like a snake, dropping Steve. The sticks clattered across marble.

The old man shook it off like someone half his age. He sprang back to his feet, a knot forming on his forehead.

"Come on, old man," the young tengu said swinging the chain in a figure eight arc.

The sound hypnotic.

Whump.

Whump.

Whump.

Without hesitation, Steve stepped forward into the eye of the storm, his hand extended.

Murphy gasped. Steve was a goner.

Instead of taking a bludgeoning, Steve negated the deadly dervish of the manriki with just an outstretched hand.

He didn't take control of the weapon, instead he allowed all his chi energy to flow into his hands until they glowed. At least Murphy thought he saw a glow. Then Steve threw a succession of straight blast chain punches, too many for Murphy to see let alone count.

The tengu, unable to deal with the pressure, stepped back in a straight line. Extending his arm again, Steve threw one final blow: a palm heel strike. It knocked the young tengu back. The tengu hit the floor and slid. The wall stopped his momentum. The tengu was now out like a light.

"Damn!" was all Murphy could say. And so, he said it again. "Damn!"

Chapter Fifty-Five

As suddenly as it began, the gunfire ceased.

"What are you waiting for?" Hayden called out. "Let's get inside."

Love seemed dazed for a second, then shook it off.

"You heard Hayden," Love said. "Let's move, people!"

Hayden followed them into the mansion, his revolver drawn, letting Love and his crew take the lead.

Love's team made quick work of the downstairs, clearing room by room, grabbing any stragglers, disarming them, cuffing both hands and feet to keep them from getting away and then leaving them for later removal. He saw no demons, just normal human beings in Sho's service. Demons or no demons, this would make a great book. Maybe another *New York Times* Best Seller!

The second floor stood abandoned. They swept the area but found no one.

On the third floor, they had to step over half a dozen dead bodies and puddles of blood. Bagging, tagging, and photographing the scene would be a nightmare.

Further down the hall, a big, long-haired Samoan had taken a knee, holding his ears, blood trickling in-between his fingers.

A smaller spiky haired guy writhed on the floor in a stupor.

"Get your hands up!" Love screamed, pointing his shotgun at the three men congregated at the end of the hall.

"We're friends of Vance Palladian," the black man, covered in plaster and blood, said, holding his hands high. "We're backing him up. You want the demons on the floor."

"Put down the shotgun!" Love said, looking directly at the young man.

"Yes, sir," the young man said, slowly lowering it to the floor.

"Okay, who am I dealing with?" Love asked.

"Paul Christian Davidson, sir," the young man said. "Veteran, U.S. Army."

"Andre Murphy, private investigator."

"Steve Chen—waiter."

If the set of circumstances weren't so bleak, Hayden might have laughed.

"If they're here with Vance," Hayden said, "they're on the right side."

"I'll take your word for it," Love said, then he turned back to Murphy and his team. "Anyone else with you?"

"No," Murphy said. "Good men are hard to find."

"I hear that. See any other perps?"

"The ones on the roof who fired at you are dead," Paul said.

"Then you have our thanks. Officer Finnegan and Puja, secure the prisoners. Then escort our friends here out of the premises," Love said. He paused a moment for emphasis. "They were never here."

As Finnegan and Puja approached, the spiky-haired one sprang to his feet, vaulting over the bigger man.

Puja hit him in the face with the butt of her rifle.

"Go back to sleep," she said. And he did.

The bigger demon grabbed Puja's rifle and tossed her. She landed on her back, sucking wind. Then he grabbed Finnegan and flung him into the wall, creating another depression in the plaster.

Officer Anderson threw down his shotgun, lowered his head, and ran for the tackle. Anderson sacked him. The Samoan flipped over Anderson's back, slapping out with one arm to dissipate the impact as he hit the floor.

Retreating into a darkened room, the Samoan looked for a tactical advantage. Anderson followed.

They grappled for dominance.

Love raised his shotgun, trying to get a bead on the Samoan. His next shot was a slug.

Anderson raised his foot, propping it on the Samoan's hip. Then he dropped to the floor in a classic Judo tomo nage, kicking the man over him, tossing him through a window.

Love blasted the Samoan and he plummeted to the pavement.

"If you're done messing around with the prisoners," Hayden said to Love's crew as they brushed themselves off, "we have to get to the teahouse."

Chapter Fifty-Six

Keikan pushed Jade through the entrance. The dojo lay empty and in shadow. Keikan walked in behind her. He heard a muffled volley of gunfire in the distance. Distracted, someone twisted the shotgun from his grip.

"What are you doing, Vance?" Keikan said when he saw who had taken his weapon.

"Sorry, Keikan," Vance said.

The lights snapped on.

"Gentlemen," Sho said, holding a pistol steady and ready. Dressed in black, he looked the part of the wise old wizard. "Time to finish the prophecy."

"Throw down the shotgun, Vance," Sho commanded.

Vance tossed it to the tatami.

"Sit down, sis," Keikan said, pushing her to the floor by the wall. Jade cursed him.

"She is no longer your sister," Sho said. "You no longer have a family."

Sho tossed a sheathed sword to Vance, and then one to Keikan.

"This is where we settle everything. Unless you want me to kill you both."

Chapter Fifty-Seven

"We don't have to do this, Vance," Keikan said softly. "He can't get both of us."

Vance examined the sword and smiled. He had an idea that could work. If not, Sho would kill whoever remained, anyway.

"No, I think we do. This is the only way," Vance said, flicking the scabbard from his blade.

The scabbard hit Keikan in the face, stunning him. He stumbled away.

Keikan drew his own sword, tossed the scabbard to the floor.

"I guess my dad didn't teach you sword fighting," Keikan said, seeing Vance's unorthodox sword handling. "Or this."

Keikan transformed, wings ripping through the back of his shirt. He lashed out with his blade.

Vance parried Keikan's blow, using the side of the sword. Transforming automatically.

Then they were in the air, two demonic visages circling and striking. Steel sparking against steel, the clang echoing throughout the dojo.

It was all Vance could do to parry each blow. He had to do something quickly.

With both feet, Vance kicked out, knocking Keikan to the floor. He landed just as Keikan rose.

Stepping on Keikan's foot, shifting his weight, he pushed him back to the floor.

Vance stood above him; swords still connected. Vance unsheathed the hidden knife from the *saya* handle.

Keikan gasped. The sword tip trained on his heart.

"Finish him, Mr. Palladian," Sho said. "Or I'll finish you both!"

"You know, Sho," Vance said. "You were right. I am going to save your daughter—"

Vance tossed the knife.

The blade sailed through the air and plunged into Sho's throat, impaling him.

"—From you!"

Stumbling back, Sho's mouth yawned open in horror, blood flooding over his lips. A terrible gurgling as he tried to breathe.

Dropping his sword, Keikan squatted. He drew his backup weapon and fired, putting Sho out of his misery.

The spell broken with Sho's death, Vance and Keikan returned to human form.

Vance's ears rang, but he still heard Jade scream.

"No!"

Keikan returned to his feet, his expression unreadable.

Then Vance watched in slow motion as Jade slipped her arms over her feet, freeing them from behind her back while still in manacles.

She retrieved her brother's sword.

As Keikan turned, she plunged the blade up and in, piercing his heart.

Vance screamed as blood bubbled over Keikan's lips.

Jade vaulted and rolled, grabbed the shotgun, took aim, and pulled the trigger.

Vance felt a sickening thwack to his skull, accompanied by a jolt of pain. Then everything went black.

Chapter Fifty-Eight

Light returned before sound. Vance stared down a long tunnel and saw a benign face on the other side. Perhaps he had died and some angelic being was welcoming him home.

The being moved its lips, but Vance couldn't hear what he was saying. Then slowly, the shaft widened, and sound returned.

The pain came back, a thumping ache on the right side of his forehead. He lay on the dojo floor, looking up at George Hayden.

A tactical team stood behind Hayden in relief.

"Vance, can you hear me?" Hayden asked. His voice sounded gentle, grandfatherly.

"Where's Jade?" Vance asked. Hayden touched his chest to keep him from rising.

"She escaped," Hayden said.

"Did she kill Keikan?" the one that looked like a leader asked.

The memory of Keikan's death hit him, made him feel sick.

He looked over to see Keikan's body draped with a tarp. Still. Lifeless. Beyond him, he saw Sho's tarp covered body. Now together forever in death.

How could she kill her own brother in cold blood? He couldn't wrap his mind around the callousness of it all.

"I don't remember," Vance said, wondering why he was protecting her.

"You got cracked pretty good by a beanbag load. I'm surprised you remember your name."

Vance held up his hands, looked at them.

"You're back to normal," Hayden said. "Keikan told me that if Sho left the property or died, the ability to transform would go with him. Something to do with ancient magic or some such. But mums the word. Don't want to end up babysat by white coats."

"Help me up," Vance said to Hayden.

"Not a good idea," Hayden said in his best grandfatherly voice. "The EMTs have a stretcher."

"I want to walk out of here."

"Okay," Hayden said. "Take it slow."

Vance rose gingerly, ignoring the headache slowly building. Hayden draped a blanket around his shoulders.

They all exited the dojo together.

The clouds had fled, and the pregnant moon now lit the darkness a bluish-purple.

They trudged down the hill toward the mansion. SWAT vans, ambulances, and police cars awaited, parked helter-skelter in the circular driveway, painting the area in garish light. Hayden's Crown Vic and an SUV stood among them, looking like they'd been through a war.

"It's just like Keikan to leave me to deal with the aftermath," Hayden said, snorting sardonically as he placed a gentle hand on Vance's back.

When they reached the mansion, a blonde female officer stood by a cruiser. Sapphire sat in back. She looked at him without expression.

Another cop pushed a cuffed Golden Dragon into the back of a different cruiser. The Golden Dragon looked worse for wear.

Vance wondered how long they'd spend in prison and what they'd do once they got out. With Sho's death, they had all lost the ability to transform.

The same couldn't be said for The Ninth God. Even under the tarp, Vance could recognize his enormous frame.

"I have something for you," Hayden said quietly as he ferreted him away from the other officers. Hayden brought him over to the tailgate of an ambulance and motioned for him to sit.

"Do you still have the banking card?" Hayden asked.

Vance searched his pockets, held up the plastic card.

"Keikan set up an account," Hayden said, handing him a slip of paper. "He transferred a bunch of Sho's money into it. I wrote down all the information. Grab it as soon as possible. No one will notice for a day or two. After that, you won't be able to access the funds."

"Thank you, detective," Vance said. "Can I give you a finder's fee?"

"No need," Hayden said. "It's about time I cash in my retirement. This job has cost me too much."

"There's something else I'd like. A souvenir. A reminder."

"Just tell me what you want, and I'll get it for you."

Two EMTs arrived.

"Take care of yourself, Vance," Hayden said with a wink. Then the older man turned and approached the blonde officer. He put his hand on her shoulder and whispered in her ear. She broke down then. Vance felt too numb to cry, but it would all catch up with him soon.

Chapter Fifty-Nine

"Let me remind you how this is going to go," Providence Police Chief Hunter Clemens said. He stood next to his contemporary, the chief of police for Newport, Larry Ernest. Both displayed their finest dress uniforms.

Beyond the twelve-foot double doors of City Hall, overlooking Kennedy Plaza, a throng of reporters waited to get the scoop.

Vance stood with Murphy, Paul, and Steve. All decked out in their best suits. To their right, Love, Puja, Anderson, and Finnegan wore dress blues with caps to match. Hayden stood to their left in his usual frumpy suit. Beside him, Officer Stacy Pepper, also in uniform, seemed to hold up despite her loss.

Vance felt bad for her, but she was young. She would eventually heal and move on with her life.

"You will march out there, keep your mouths shut, and play heroes," Chief Clemens said. "Do not answer questions, and you best *remember* the *official story*.

"You were all a part of a joint taskforce *authorized* and coordinated to take down the Maramoto organization. As soon as Vance discovered the illegal activity, he liaised with Detective Keikan and acted as informant. He *did not* take part in anything illicit. All suspects have been arrested. The estate will go up for auction. Neat and tidy."

"And you, Hayden," the chief said, stepping close to him. "You will not write a book about this."

The chief didn't wait for Hayden's reply.

"Now go and accept your medals."

Vance followed the two chiefs as they burst through the doors and onto the grand staircase.

Vance took a deep breath and emerged into daylight, his friend by his side and Keikan's team behind him. Cameras flashed as the press swarmed around them.

Chapter Sixty

"I'll have another," Murphy said as he cut a second slice of birthday cake. He withdrew the samurai sword server, wiped it off with a napkin, sheathed it in his obi belt, and then bowed.

"You're going to get fat," Vance said, shaking his head.

"Don't I know it?" Murphy said, patting his tummy before digging in.

Children hollered in the background as a young lady Vance hired, an early childhood education teacher he had taught basic Tae Kwon Do, led an introduction to martial arts class.

The kids always wanted cake first, and the parents were happy to stuff their faces with frosting. Frosting, a salve to training, and screaming kids.

So far, not one child had vomited. Vance counted himself lucky. He also felt lucky that both his senior student, Tim Mancuso, and his favorite young student, Sara Brody, had returned to regular classes.

"You know, I just might marry that bad girl I was telling you about before all this craziness happened."

"Thought she broke up with you." Vance said.

"I broke up with her," Murphy corrected. "Think that was a mistake. Marriage would give me a license to get fat."

"And go bald," Vance added.

"Yeah, that too," Murphy said, then shoveled another bite of cake. When he finished chewing, he said, "So, you finally went all the way with the commercial dojo."

"You don't approve?"

"On the contrary, my good man. I think this school might keep you out of trouble," Murphy said. "What the hell is that?"

Murphy pointed at a tengu mask resting on a pedestal by the far wall. It looked out of place with the modern equipment, including the Little Dragon Romper Room stuff—all courtesy of the Maramoto organization's money.

"That's a souvenir from another time and place," Vance said, returning Murphy's wink. "Let me show you something."

They walked away from the party, Murphy still eating his cake, and went into Vance's office, just off the main training area.

"Impressive," Murphy said, pointing his fork at two new diplomas on the wall. He must have seen Susan's photo in between the framed rank certificates but didn't mention it.

"I finally sucked it up, went to another teacher, and got my fourth Dan in Tae Kwon Do. It was a pain in the ass."

"I'm sure it was," Murphy said. "I was going to ask you about that new highfalutin master belt."

"Yeah, well, nobody's really a master of anything."

"Ain't that the truth."

"He also ranked me in Hapkido based on Sho's Jujutsu teachings," Vance said.

"You could have come to me," Murphy said, holding back a smirk.

"Yeah, I don't think I want you as my teacher," Vance said, laughing. "No offense."

"None taken," Murphy said, holding up his hands. "I don't blame you. But listen, if it ever becomes too hard to make a living teaching these tykes, or you want to moonlight, I'm starting my own PI business. I put the time in to get my license. So, I figured, what the hell. And I got this feisty chick to come play receptionist. It's good to be me."

Murphy handed Vance his new card, and Vance was glad to take it. Who knew what the future held?

They exited the office just as Hayden entered the school.

Hayden carried a picture frame in his left hand. He had a messenger bag slung over his right shoulder, and it looked like he was wearing the same suit he always wore. Maybe he had a closet full of them like Einstein.

Hayden didn't bother kicking off his shoes, and Vance couldn't bring himself to chastise him.

"Good to see you guys," Hayden said. They shook hands. Hayden looked around, shuffled his feet.

"What have you got there?" Vance asked.

"Oh, this is Keikan's Dojo Kun or something. His guidelines for living and training. He'd want you to have it."

Hayden handed over the Dojo Kun to him. Vance sniffed back a well of emotion.

"I have a great spot right here," Vance said as they walked further into the dojang. "Nails in the wall and everything." He hung it up, and they were quiet for a moment, reverent.

The sound of the children's training receded. Keikan would always have a voice as long as Vance's students read his words.

Hayden cleared his throat and the moment of silence ended.

"Oh, that reminds me," Hayden said, pulling a trade paperback from his satchel. "It's an ARC, an Advanced Reader Copy. Wanted you to have it. I even signed it."

Vance read the title.

The Kaiden: Secret Soldiers of the Maramoto Crime Family.

"Didn't the Chief tell you—?"

"I didn't mention the Tengu. Besides, I've never been good at listening," Hayden said, and they all laughed.

Chapter Sixty-One

Time passed quickly as Vance built his business. Memories of his time with Sho and Jade faded by sheer force of will. Nothing remained now except for a relic and the techniques Sho taught him. Vance had done his best to expunge them of evil and pass them on to his students.

After the last class ended, he remained to complete the day's paperwork.

As he was about to leave, headlights pierced the slatted blinds on the windows, projecting a line of shadows across the matted floor.

A car pulled into the parking lot. Maybe a student had forgotten something, or Murphy had stopped in to buy him a beer. Vance waited. He heard car doors close, but the engine never shut off. Then he caught movement through the openings in the blinds.

Three men wearing demon masks and dark suits burst through the unlocked door.

Vance's heart accelerated, but he stood like a mountain, unmovable, waiting for them to make the first move.

The demons stood their ground.

A woman entered—Jade.

She wore a kimono that contrasted with the demon's modern business attire.

"How have you been, Vance?" Jade asked. Her voice smiled, but she did not.

"I was doing well," Vance said, assuming a fighting stance, looking from one demon to the next.

"Wait for me outside," she said to the demons. They looked at her silently, cocking their heads. "You heard me."

They didn't hesitate further.

As the demons exited, Vance's heart slowed to normal, but he remained on guard.

Jade sauntered over to the pedestal that held the tengu mask.

"I see you took a souvenir from my father's office," Jade said as she walked from the display.

"A trophy from another time," Vance said.

"Yes, it certainly is," Jade said, then turned to him. "I want you back, Vance."

He could see the longing in her eyes, that deep ache that matched what he felt inside.

"After what I did to your family?" Vance asked.

"It was my father's destiny to die," Jade said. "And my destiny to take his place."

She walked now past his office and stared at the Dojo Kun her brother had penned.

"Why didn't you turn me in?" Jade asked as she sauntered toward the entryway.

"I don't know," Vance said. And it was the truth.

She turned around, untied the obi, and pulled the kimono off her shoulders, exposing her naked back. Green and black tattoos scrawled over her svelte form, snaking all the way to the cleft in her bottom.

"All that was my father's can be yours, Vance," she said, her voice musical. "The estate is back in my hands. It's amazing what money can do, along with information on the right people.

"The tattoo, once complete, will give me my father's power but bind me to the estate.

"Come back. Take what is rightfully yours."

The yearning for that type of life, that much power, still pulled at him. How easy it would be to throw off the reins of society and take control of the Kaiden. But even the power could not eclipse how much he wanted her now.

He shook his head, regained his senses.

"I can't," Vance said. "I've chosen to return to my old path."

"A pity," Jade said, as she tied the kimono in place. She turned to face him. "If you come back, I might even be willing to share you with Sapphire, when she gets out of prison, of course."

"I've already given you my answer," Vance said.

"Just remember, you're always welcome," Jade said as she turned around, pulling her long, lustrous hair from across her face with one carefully practiced move. "I will always take you back."

He knew she would, and he'd spend the rest of his life resisting the urge to return to her.

"When you shot me?" Vance asked. "Did you know the shotgun was loaded with non-lethal loads?"

She gave him a sly smile, turned on her heels, and walked out into the night.

Vance traversed to the window and opened the blinds fully. He watched as a masked demon opened the car door for her. She gave Vance one last look before the door closed and hid her behind tinted glass.

He watched as the limo pulled out of the parking area and back onto the street, headed for the Maramoto estate in Newport.

Vance returned to the display. He stared longingly at the mask, the ghoulish countenance, the reflection of the true face he held within.

Then, without another thought, he turned away from the display and shut off the lights.

Meet the Author

DAVID NORTH-MARTINO is the author of YEAR OF THE DEMON (Crossroad Press) and WOLVES OF VENGEANCE. His short fiction has appeared in numerous fiction venues including *Epitaphs: The Journal of the New England Horror Writers* (Shroud Publishing), Daughters of Icarus: *New Feminist Science Fiction and Fantasy* (Pink Narcissus Press), and *The Horror Zine's Book of Werewolf Stories* (Hellhound Books Publishing). A graduate of the University of Massachusetts, he holds a BLA in English and psychology. When he's not writing, David enjoys studying and teaching martial arts. You can also hear him co-host The House of Mystery Radio Show on NBC News Radio KCAA 106.5 FM Los Angeles and on podcast. He lives with his supportive wife and a needy tuxedo cat in a small town in Massachusetts.

Website
https://davidnorthmartino.com

Facebook
https://www.facebook.com/dnorthmartino/

Twitter/X
https://twitter.com/dnorthmartino

YouTube
https://www.youtube.com/channel/UCWAGfK61_Pc6vOlOmUD1sRg

TikTok
https://www.tiktok.com/@dnorthmartino

Instagram
https://www.instagram.com/dnorthmartino/

Curious about other Crossroad Press books? Stop by our website:
http://crossroadpress.com
We offer quality writing
in digital, audio, and print formats.

Subscribe to our newsletter on the website homepage and receive a
free eBook.